The Yearbook

My name is David Kallas.

I am in trouble.

I do not know how long I will live.

My only possessions are the clothes I'm wearing and my backpack, which contains this pen and pad.

I do not know if my mother and my house still exist.

I need to piece it all together. To start from the beginning. At the very least, the writing will keep me sane.

More importantly, there will be a record. Someone will know what happened here. And someone will *need* to know. Because it all may happen again.

And when it does, there may not be anyone left.

Look out for:

The Forbidden Game I:
The Hunter
L J Smith

Thirteen Again
Various

The Mall
Richie Tankersley Cusick

Nightmare Hall:
The Scream Team
Diane Hoh

Point Horror
THE YEARBOOK

Peter Lerangis

■ SCHOLASTIC

For Tina,
at long last

Scholastic Children's Books,
7-9 Pratt Street, London NW1 0AE, UK
a division of Scholastic Publications Ltd
London ~ New York ~ Toronto ~ Sydney ~ Auckland

First published in the US by Scholastic Inc, 1994
First published in the UK by Scholastic Publications Ltd, 1995

Copyright © Peter Lerangis, 1994

ISBN 0 590 55903 6

Printed by Cox and Wyman Ltd, Reading, Berks

10 9 8 7 6 5 4

Prologue

My name is David Kallas.

I am in trouble.

I do not know how long I will live.

My only possessions are the clothes I'm wearing and my backpack, which contains this pen and pad.

I do not know if my mother and my house still exist.

What's more, I have a splitting headache.

But let's look on the bright side.

I am alone with Ariana Maas. I am too embarrassed to say *exactly* how that makes me feel. She is smart and gorgeous and kind and thoughtful, and she has a body to *die* for — which I am reminded of only because our clothes happen to be tattered in some convenient places. We are alone on top of a hill outside Wetherby, Massachusetts, without anyone around for miles. Unfortunately, Ariana is fast asleep. She's also sucking her thumb and muttering. This is not normal for her (I don't think), but under the circumstances, I can't blame her.

Which brings me to the minus side: I believe I have destroyed my entire hometown. This, of course, weighs heavily on my mind. It's a big thing for a seventeen-year-old to do, possibly a first. I think, however, it's too late to put it on my college applications.

The smoke is still billowing below us. It looks as if we'll be up here a long time. I feel numb and nauseous.

I need to piece it all together. To start from the beginning. At the very least, the writing will keep me sane.

More importantly, there will be a record. Someone will know what happened here.

And someone *will* need to know. Because it all may happen again.

And when it does, there may not be anyone left.

PART ONE

David

Chapter 1

I will begin with what I saw on the night of April 15. But, first, a word from your narrator.

I, David Kallas, am a Genius.

This is not a boast. I don't look or talk anything like a Genius. My grades are pretty mediocre, and I have a lazy streak from here to Montana.

But my test scores confirm it: *IQ Level — Genius*. Right up there with *Hair and Eyes — Brown* and *Height — 5'11"*. So I don't fight it.

What does it mean to be a Genius? It means teachers always look at you perplexed and disappointed. It means every adult you're in contact with thinks he or she must be doing something wrong. It means *you* must be doing something wrong, because you're exactly like everybody else.

For a Genius, I did an extremely stupid thing on April 15. Now, I could have detected warning signs, as early as February, but I'll go into that later. Anyway, on that night, I took a walk in the Ramble.

The Ramble is a small forest at the edge of town, sloping downward into a wimpy river called the Wampanoag. A few well-worn footpaths wind through the trees, and one path of tire tracks leads to a secluded clearing. To many people in my drab hometown of Wetherby, Massachusetts, the Ramble is *Nature*. To others, especially those who know the clearing well, the Ramble is *Sex*.

I'll put it more delicately. As a teenager in Wetherby, book-learning goes on in school. Learning about everything else happens in the Ramble.

Parents warn their kids never to go there after dark. The older the kid, the more frequent the warnings. Once puberty hits, it becomes the world's most dangerous place. Oddly enough, no one can actually recall a crime there in years. You are more likely to come upon a parked car with steamed-up windows than a mugger.

Well, I did come upon one of those cars that fateful night. And Ariana Maas was in it. With someone who was not me.

I admit, I asked for it. I kind of thought she'd

be there. I was on a very indirect route to the print shop to proofread our high school yearbook, the Wetherby *Voyager*. I guess my curiosity had gotten the worst of me.

Her thick red hair was unmistakable, even mashed against the mousy brown hair of her boyfriend, Smut. (Yes, Smut. The initials stand for *S*tephen *M*atthew *U*nderwood-*T*aylor.) I had an urge to pull open the car door and yank the guy out. But I didn't.

I may be a Genius, but I'm not a Hero.

I slunk away before they could see me. If I had had a tail, it would have been between my legs. Ariana was discovering heaven in a Chevy, while I was off to check for apostrophes. What a life.

The weather had been horrendous for months, so the river was pretty swollen. It wasn't the measly sewage-choked trickle we'd all come to know and love. I decided to follow it to the other side of the Ramble. That would put me on the road to Someday My Prints Will Come, which I think is the dumbest name for a print shop ever invented.

That was when I saw the brownish lump of fur. It was floating on the water, mostly hidden by a boulder.

At first I thought it was a badger, or a river

rat. I was still angry and frustrated and hurt, thinking about Ariana, and that is the only explanation I can give for what I did next.

I picked up a rock and tiptoed closer. Being quiet was easy. After all the recent storms, the fallen branches were soggy, and the ground soft.

Slowly I made my way around the boulder. The critter was still, sleeping maybe. Easy target.

I cocked my arm, took aim, and threw.

Thud. Dead on. Right in the critter's side.

I braced for a yelp or a scream. If the thing came after me, I would need to book.

But the rock bounced silently away. It left a small indentation in the flesh. I slumped and sighed. Hooray for me. I'd hit a dead rat.

I stepped out from behind the boulder, feeling extremely stupid. Now I got a closer look at the fur.

It wasn't fur.

Fur was not that long. Not on any animal you'd find in the Ramble.

But it couldn't be what I thought it was. The body — the *object* — covered with this hairy substance, was almost flat. As if it had been stepped on. As if it were a thick, wet mask, not a living thing.

I noticed the smell then. Not an ugly smell,

but sort of chalky and slightly sweet, like dried milk.

Leave.

Leave now.

My brain echoed with that warning. Did I listen? *Noooo.*

I kept walking around the boulder. I reached down and pulled the brown hair ball toward me. Why? I'm still asking myself.

I should have taken a look at the whole thing before I touched it, but I didn't. Only when I had a fistful of hair was I angled close enough to see the whole body. Only then did I realize it was human.

My hand froze. I felt something shoot through me, like an electric jolt. The smell was overpowering now.

When I yanked my hand away, the face lolled around. It was a young face, familiar somehow. But there was no way on earth I could tell who it was.

A scream caught in my throat. I wanted to run, but I couldn't move. My eyes were locked on the corpse.

Under an outfit of black pants and a shirt, it was grotesque, distorted. It bent to the right and left, not at the joints, but everywhere. Its calves curved into the opening of a drainage pipe, bending forward in a smooth and perfect

C shape, opposite to the way the knees were supposed to bend. Like a Gumby.

A Gumby? A vicious laugh welled up inside me. But I didn't open my mouth for fear that all my sanity would go rushing out. I just kept staring.

Then, for the first time in my life, I fainted.

Chapter 2

Out of the darkness comes a dream.

In my dream I'm a man and I'm fishing in the river and I catch a whopping bluefish. I reel it in, and it's flipping, flopping, desperate to get back into the water. But my hook is clean through its mouth, and blood sprays all over the place with each flip.

I want to throw it back, but a little boy comes up to me, screaming happily. He wants to take it home, which means I have to clean it.

I drop the fishing rod, grab the fish's tail with one hand, and take out a gutting knife with the other. All I need to do is slit open the belly, pull out the guts, and throw the fish in my pail.

I've done this a million times, but this time I start to feel sick. The fish is enormous, and as I cut it open, thick warm blood spurts into my face. I grit my teeth and grab its insides. They are throbbing. I pull, and pull, and pull, and pull. The entrails seem endless, but they're attached to the bones, so I keep pulling. The skeleton is now coming out and I'm thinking: great, instant fillet. The little boy is staring, horrified.

That is when I realize the fish is not a fish. It's a classmate of mine, and he's screaming for me to stop.

Chapter 3

I did not reach the printer that night. That much I remember.

My nightmare jarred me awake into a pitch-black night.

The first thing I noticed was the strange, chalky smell. I started shaking, and it had little to do with the freezing temperature. Panic was stealing heat from my body, sending pinpricks of ice through me. I could not see the river, but I could hear it, maybe two feet away. I had been lying next to the . . . the what? The body? The *hide*? I didn't know how to think of it.

I bolted to my feet. I did not look back as I ran blindly away from the Wampanoag River.

The rest is fragments, flashes of memory. I've forgotten the *physical* part of my trip home — as if my mind had separated from the rest of my body, floating outside it, letting my legs stumble over the ground. Thoughts spat themselves into my consciousness, and my brain tried frantically to digest them.

It wasn't until I'd arrived home that I realized my pants were muddy and wet. I ran straight into the bathroom, stripped, and turned on the shower.

"David!" my mother shouted through the closed door. "Where were you?"

What was I supposed to tell her? *Nothing, Ma. Just a quiet evening in the Ramble, spying on some taboo behavior, then having a nap next to a hollowed-out human. Oh, and by the way, I need to wash my pants out.*

Uh-huh. Right.

I wished my dad were alive. He would have believed every word, and insisted on going back with me. Then he would have talked about it for months, embellishing the story each time.

"Proofreading the yearbook!" I replied. "Remember I called you?"

"Until one in the morning?"

"Sorry. I lost track."

Don't get me wrong. Mom is cool. But she has this proper, old-fashioned streak. Her parents immigrated to Wetherby from Greece. She was not allowed to wear pants to school, or marry a non-Greek, or work for a living. That last part changed when my dad died of a heart attack. For the last seven years, she's been working at a paper-tubing factory.

Mom had all kinds of names for dad. When he got into his frequent story-telling moods, he was Homer, after the ancient Greek narrator. When he dressed up, he was Adonis, the handsomest Greek god. When he sang, he was Apollo, the god of music (although he sounded like Jerry Lewis on a bad day). When he was mad, he became Zeus.

Too bad she wasn't right. If he were a god, he could come down and explain what I had seen in the Ramble.

I threw my pants in the sink. Then I turned the shower up to full blast and hopped in.

The water sent red rivulets down my calves, cleaning out a bruised crosshatch of cuts and scrapes on my legs.

The shower water was soothing. The harsh bathroom light flooded my mind with rationality: The body wasn't real. Couldn't have been. It was a mannequin, a latex dummy. Stolen from a store window as a prank. That was it.

Simple.

But there were a few problems. Mannequins didn't have skin. And fingernails and eyes. They were not squishy and caved in. The one in the river wouldn't have sold too many clothes.

It was real.

I had seen a dead body.

I knew I was different now. Changed forever. All because of this one event. And it wasn't just what I had seen. Something had gotten inside me; I could feel it. Something cold and sticky and slightly nauseating. Could fear itself take root in a person's body, like a virus?

At that moment, I hated Ariana. Hated her for making me want her so much. *That* was the reason I had joined the yearbook in the first place. If I hadn't done that, I'd never have gotten stuck with proofreading, never seen the body. I'd be the same happy but screwed-up kid I'd always been.

Which brings me to the beginning of this whole fiasco. The day I met Ariana.

The day of the Great Wetherby Earthquake.

Chapter 4

Now, I know earthquakes are no big deal in some places, like California. But they are in New England. They just don't happen. We are not in the "earthquake belt."

Well, the belt was loosened on a gray and windy afternoon in February. The seventh, to be exact. I was walking home from school the fun way. Fun because Ariana Maas was a half-block in front of me. (If you could see her body move, you'd know what I mean. Real slow and lazylike, with lots of . . . well, movement.)

Sounds pathetic, I know. But I was obsessed, okay? Don't tell me you don't know what that feels like.

It started when she looked at me with her hazel-green eyes in the school cafeteria. It was in November, I think. I was mopping up this chocolate shake I had spilled, and when I glanced up, she was watching, with kind of a sneer. There's this scene in *Dr. Zhivago* where the two lovers see each other on a trolley for the first time. Suddenly the camera cuts to sparks on the electric wires overhead (duh, get the message?). Well, that's how it felt when Ariana looked at me. Only the sparks were DC, not AC. They went only one way.

I vaguely knew she was editor in chief of the *Voyager*, and that Smut was an editor, too. Smut, by the way, is six two and 180 pounds. He also finished seventh in our class (out of 179), was a wide receiver on the football team, played the lead in the school production of *Carousel*, got into Yale early admissions, and is friendly to everyone.

You can see why I hate him.

It was a warm afternoon for midwinter. As Ariana crossed Cass Street, the wind tossed her thick hair like flickering flames. Cass borders the Ramble, and its trees were bending and groaning in the gusts. Chipmunks chittered, birds argued, crows cawed and traced crazy patterns overhead. The Wampanoag River, which is pretty far in from the road, sounded like a crashing surf.

When I heard thunder, I said good-bye to Ariana in my mind and began to hightail it home before the storm.

I didn't get far.

The world went suddenly silent. Like a pulled plug on a stereo. Absolute nothingness. You never know how *loud* plain old nature is until it shuts up.

The woods were motionless, the sky blank and gray as slate.

I stopped in my tracks. I could see Ariana looking toward the Ramble, then toward me. I quickly tried to think of something clever to say.

When my knees buckled, I thought it was nerves. Then I felt a vague queasiness. Around me, things got blurry then sharp again, as if some giant were twanging the world like a guitar string. I heard a low rumbling underground that reminded me of the Boston subway. Finally everything sort of *jittered*, side to side, and I felt as if I were a fly on the back of an angry nine-acre bull.

I ran to the nearest tree, as if holding it would somehow stabilize me.

The silence broke with a cracking sound, like a bat hitting a baseball.

Then Ariana screamed, "Look out!"

I felt a blow to my chest. My feet flew out from beneath me. I tumbled to the ground, my face buried in the folds of a pink-and-turquoise L.L. Bean anorak.

I was flat on my back, my body wrapped up

in Ariana's. It was a moment I'd dreamed about for months. I'd planned it, rehearsed every word I'd say, every move I'd make. I should have been prepared.

"Oww — " was my clever opening line.

"Sorry," Ariana said, untangling herself. "Are you okay?"

"Yeah, I think."

We both stood up and brushed ourselves off. I felt stable again. A bird screeched, and I saw a squirrel making agitated circles in the woods. Behind Ariana an enormous branch rocked slowly on the pavement, leafless and broken off at one end.

It was lying right where I'd been standing.

"Oh my God, you saved my life," I said.

Ariana smiled at me, and I felt a second earthquake. This one started inside me, and stayed there. "That was amazing, huh?" she remarked. "I wonder how strong it was — like on the Richter scale."

I shrugged. "I don't think they make them out here."

"What?"

"Richter scales."

Ariana laughed. I nearly had a heart attack, it sounded so beautiful.

Rain had started to fall, heavier by the second. "Come on over to my house," Ariana said, turning to go. "You can fix your hand up there."

I looked down and noticed for the first time that the palm of my left hand resembled freshly chopped hamburger.

I ran after her, my blood pounding. All right, an invitation inside for a Band-Aid wasn't exactly a moonlight skinny-dip on a Mexican beach, but it was a start. I had to take what I could get.

After I was bandaged up, Mr. and Mrs. Maas invited me to stay for dinner, but I felt too nervous. If Smut showed up, he might get the wrong idea, and I didn't want to end up on the wrong end of a carving knife. So I politely refused.

As Ariana and I passed through the living room to the front door, her mom, dad, and younger sister were staring at the TV.

". . . Damage to area homes, as far as we know, was limited to a few broken plates and glasses in private homes," the announcer was saying. "At 5.1 on the Richter scale, the quake would seem mild to a San Franciscan, but it baffles local experts. It far surpassed the tremor felt in this area in 1950. Is there an active fault below Wetherby? Impossible, says Dr. Paul Bascomb, of the County Meteorological Institute. But don't try to tell that to the students of Wetherby High School. . . ."

The camera cut to our school. An ancient maple tree was lying across the front lawn, its top branches embedded in a parked car.

The Maases all gasped. But Ariana smiled and blurted out, "Hey, we've got an event!"

"Ssshh," her sister said.

I must have been giving Ariana a weird look, because she immediately turned to me and explained in a whisper, "I mean, for the yearbook. Every year we have a theme, based on some major event. We try to tie all the aspects of the yearbook together with it. We can have an earthquake theme!"

I thought it was a dumb idea. "Great idea," I said.

"Only problem is, I have to find another staff member. Sonya Eggert was supposed to work on the theme, but she moved." Then, for the first time, Ariana looked at me with something like interest. "Do you write, David?"

I'll give you three guesses what my answer was.

And that is how I joined the Wetherby High School yearbook. As something called Theme Coordinator.

I was in charge of a little one-page introduction to the book, blurbs and funny captions about the earthquake, and appropriate photos.

Me, who had never gotten higher than a "Shows Improvement" on any English paper in my life.

I didn't care. I was going to spend a large part of the rest of the year with Ariana. Smut or no Smut.

Chapter 5

"Smiling or serious?" asked Mark "Rosie" Rosenthal, the *Voyager* photo editor. He peered at me through his Minolta.

It was an April morning, about a week before I found the body. Rosie's basement felt like the Arctic. "Serious," I managed to croak before letting out a huge sneeze. My Groucho Marx glasses lurched down my nose. They tugged at my white fright wig, which slipped forward and unseated my hat. The hat clattered to the ground, sending a couple of plastic grapes rolling across the floor.

"You're losing fruit," said Rosie.

I scooped up the grapes and reattached them to their stem, right behind the bunch of fake bananas and to the left of an apple and a plum. "Whose idea was this, anyway?"

"Yours," Rosie replied. "Now, can we take this shot?"

"Go for it," I said.

I donned my fruit-hat, sat straight in the portrait chair, and looked at Rosie grimly through the fake glasses, nose, and mustache. He managed to get in a few shots before he exploded with laughter. Rosie is a giggler. He's constantly trying to look at the odd side of things — and he was having no trouble today.

The Bananahead was just one of my many brilliant concepts for the Wetherby *Voyager*.

You see, after Ariana had popped the fateful question to me that day in February, I had transformed. I was no longer meek and mild David Kallas. I had become Mr. Yearbook.

The *Voyager* was on a late schedule this year, because the print-shop owner was off in Tibet studying meditation till April. (Don't ask.) So for two months, I lived and breathed the yearbook. I drove Rosie crazy about getting quake photos. I infiltrated the school newspaper and convinced some of their staffers to write funny captions for us.

And when twenty-three kids didn't show up for their *Voyager* photos, and Ariana called them "bananaheads" — *voilà* — I thought of a way to get even. My plan was to put a photo of the Bananahead above each of the no-shows' names in the yearbook. Just a joke. Nothing too offensive.

Our faculty advisor, Mr. DeWaart, hated the idea. But the rest of us outvoted him.

Over the weeks, Ariana began looking at me with respect. (I would have preferred something stronger, like infatuation, but respect was fine.)

"Okay, I can't take any more," Rosie said, still red from laughter.

I pulled off my disguise. "Good. It's freezing in here. When can you have the prints?"

Rosie shrugged. "This afternoon, I guess."

"I'll come by on my way back from the library."

"The *library*? It's Saturday!"

"Hey, I have a date, okay?"

"Fine. Don't get testy. I just thought you lost your mind. I'm not the first."

"Nor the last. See you."

My date was with Edna Klatsch. She was the town librarian.

We had our rendezvous in the lobby of Lyte Memorial Library — but I had to share her with another man.

He was an artist, repairing a mural that had been damaged in the February quake when a tree fell through the glass entrance.

The painting was faded and awful. It showed a bearded white man, dressed in formal clothes, shaking hands with an African slave in front of an open trapdoor in the ground. The slave looked bewildered, and a dozen or so equally dazed-looking slave families stood behind him.

The mural was labeled JONAS LYTE, WETHERBY RESIDENT, HERO OF THE UNDERGROUND RAILROAD.

Jonas Lyte's self-satisfied smile had been turned into a white plaster gash by the fallen tree. The artist was trying to recreate it.

"You're making him into a clown!" Mrs. Klatsch scolded. Then she turned to me and said, "Hello, David. I'm very busy today. Follow me."

She led me inside, into the locked area that contained the library's rare and most-likely-to-be-stolen books.

Mrs. Klatsch raised an eyebrow. "You're looking for — ?"

"Pictures of the 1950 quake, for a 'then-and-now' feature for the yearbook," I replied.

She pointed. "Try the big maroon book. I'll be back to help you. If you steal anything, I'll have your head."

The book was called *Our Town: A Wetherby History from 1634 to the Present*. I flipped to a section on the '50 quake. The school actually had caught fire, so I could use some incredibly dramatic shots. But I loved the "candids" the most — stiff, sober-looking kids pointing to fallen trees and broken windows. High school students from 1950 all look about forty years old, I don't know why.

I kept paging through, stopping to read whatever interested me. Near the beginning, I saw something else I wanted to use. It was a drawing, labeled *Witch Hunt, Spuyten Duyvil (Wetherby), 1686*. In it, a young and innocent-looking "witch" was being burned at the stake. Next to her the devil was rising out of a crack in the ground, shrouded in mist.

"The burning of Annabelle Spicer," came a voice from behind me. "Spuyten Duyvil means 'spitting devil' in Dutch. That was the name of an area of Wetherby. Shameful . . . but rather a hilarious engraving, don't you think?"

I'd known Mrs. Klatsch was approaching before she had said those words. It was the smell of Ben-Gay, mixed with some perfume that only elderly women seem to wear. Eau de Old Lady. Mrs. Klatsch was probably not around at the founding of Wetherby, but she didn't miss it by much.

I couldn't help laughing at her comment. The

picture was pretty ridiculous. "Which area was it?"

"No one knows for sure." She took the book and leafed through. "You'll find a lot of other important things here, you know. Like Wetherby's role in the Underground Railroad during the Civil War — which will never be looked at the same way after the artist in the lobby is done. . . ." She sighed and shook her head. "We were a spy post during the Revolution, too. Lord, the Pilgrims set up the first college in the country here — but try telling that to the snobs down at Harvard. You know, we also have some wonderful microfilmed material. . . ."

Obviously Mrs. Klatsch was proud of her collection. I was impressed, too. I never expected Wetherby to have such a glamorous history.

Mr. DeWaart described my hometown best: "It's a small town, but ugly." Wetherby looked like Last Place in a town-design contest of nearsighted architects. Houses were old and drab, office buildings and stores were rundown, and the hottest nighttime hangout on Main Street was the Arby's (the Methodist church on Sundays being a close second).

But Mrs. Klatsch knew all the town's secrets, and she let me photocopy everything I needed for free.

I was there for three hours — on a Saturday, *voluntarily*. I, David Kallas, in the spring of senior year, after class ranks were set and college applications were in, and it didn't matter if I'd got a D in everything — I was *working*. It was sick.

Ariana was the cause of my disease. Or the cure. Depending on how you looked at it.

She and I worked well together — except when I wanted to use the picture of the burning of Annabelle Spicer in "Student Activities" as a joke. She thought it was sexist, and also irrelevant to the theme, even though I argued the crack in the ground looked earthquakish.

Sometimes she can be too serious.

Fortunately, that was the only blot on my record. I worked like a dog right up until D-Day.

D-Day was Deadline Day — Monday, April 11. We had to get our "mock-up" to the printer — which meant blocking where every single photo and caption was supposed to go, on cardboard sheets the size of yearbook pages. Getting this done in time was brutal. I don't think anyone did a homework assignment for weeks (except Smut, who doesn't sleep, I guess).

We finished just before midnight at Ariana's house on Sunday, April 10. Mr. DeWaart took the mock-ups and dropped them off at the printer's before the next morning.

We spent the rest of the week recovering. On Friday the fifteenth, we had a party at Mr. DeWaart's apartment.

"Abandon hope, all ye who enter!" Mr. DeWaart greeted Ariana, Smut, and me at his door. We had all come up the apartment stairs together. "Welcome to the ship of party fools!"

"Hi, Mr. DeWaart," I said.

"Say *what*?" he replied. "It's Richard to you, my boy."

"But your name is Joel."

"Details, details. Come on in."

Mr. DeWaart was weird. No question. His nickname was Wartface, because of his last name and two large moles on his right cheek and left hand. His image: tweed jackets and wrinkled shirts, a thick salt-and-pepper beard, mismatched socks, and Top-Siders. He hardly ever smiled; sometimes you didn't know he'd told a joke until about five minutes after you heard it. He'd graduated college four years earlier, which made him about twenty-five, but he looked older. He was both a genius and an awesome athlete. He coached the crew team and organized some of the team members (and other achiever types, including Smut) into a small group called "The Delphic Club," which sat around after practice and had heavy, top-secret discussions. (No one knew what they were about, or cared.) Between all that, advising the yearbook, teaching history, and working toward his Ph.D. at night, he didn't have time for much else.

Still, I figured: mid-twenties, unattached, athletic, smart — it can't be all work. I looked around for some tell-tale signs of bachelor life — cigarette butts with blood-red lipstick staining their tips, a lingering hint of feminine perfume in the bathroom, or even just a stack of dirty plates in the sink.

No such luck. He lived in a small, one-bedroom apartment with piles of books and papers in every corner, shabby furniture, and some crummy artwork on the walls — mostly pictures of ancient Greece, philosophers in togas, stuff like that. (Bo-ring.)

But, hey, a party's a party.

John Christopher, the *Voyager* sports editor, waved to us as we walked in. He was by a large fruit bowl, along with Rachel Green (our business editor) and Liz Montez (activities editor).

"Wai — her — gluzb — " John gargled, his jaw working like crazy.

A moment later, he reached into his mouth and pulled out a perfectly knotted cherry stem. With a huge, satisfied grin, he sang, "Ta-da!"

John is large and competitive. If you walk to school with him, he will not let you get there first. If you eat with him, he has to have more than you. Because of that last habit, he's too . . . *cumbersome* for most sports, so he writes about them for the school paper and the yearbook.

"You did that with just your *tongue*?" Rosie asked.

"That is gross," Liz said, her smooth, round face puckering in disgust.

John looked disappointed. "It's supposed to be sexy."

"Puh-leeze!" groaned Rachel. "Give it up."

Rachel and John have been going out for years, but you'd never know it. They're always picking on each other. Rachel's as petite as John is big. She has huge, dark eyes that can be vulnerable or furious at a moment's notice.

Of course, all the guys in the group had to try the trick. I managed to choke on my cherry stem, and Rosie chewed his into a limp string. Smut, of course, pulled out a perfect knot.

"Let me try." Ariana picked a stem and put it in her mouth. Her lips moved up and down rhythmically. Her eyes became half-lidded and mischievous. Her jaw hollowed and thickened. A tiny drop of saliva moistened the left corner of her mouth.

I thought I was going to faint.

When she took out her knotted stem, I was a basket case. I was sitting upright in a chair, but my soul had to be scraped off the floor. Eight weeks of working side by side with her had taken its toll.

"That was *great*," Smut said, grinning.

Ariana smiled. "Mmm. I know."

"Make me puke," Rachel remarked.

"Eat your heart out," John said.

"I do," Rachel retorted. "Every time I realize I'm with you."

"*Who-o-o-oa!*" cried Liz, laughing.

Ariana and Smut started giggling about something. Slowly they made their way to the couch in the corner of the living room. It was threadbare and stained, but they didn't seem to mind. They sat right down, holding hands and whispering.

Smut was lucky. If he'd been in front of an open window, I think I would have pushed him.

Rosie was in charge of the CD player, and

he put on some dance tunes. I danced a little with Rachel and Liz. But after awhile I caught a glimpse of Ariana and Smut kissing, and my motor stopped running. Liz asked me if I was okay, and I said yes, I was just tired.

But all I was thinking was: Why didn't they just go off and park somewhere? Why torment the rest of us, who had to sit and watch?

Well, maybe not the rest of us. Maybe just me. Everyone else seemed to be having a great time.

For the first time in my life I wished I had a vice, like drinking or smoking or writing terrible poetry. But I don't, so I consoled myself with elaborate murder schemes.

At one point Mr. DeWaart went into his bedroom to answer a phone call. When he came back, he turned off the CD player and announced, "Okay, listen up, guys. Time for a reality check. I just got a call from Mr. Brophy at the print shop. The proofs are ready."

"All *riiight!*" Rosie said.

"The bad news is, someone has to go check them."

A big groan went up from the room. "Tonight?" Liz asked.

"Or first thing tomorrow morning. Mr. Brophy's projects piled up while he was gone, and he'd have to put them all ahead of us if we waited. The other alternative is to let *him* do the proofreading, which I don't recommend — not with some of the last names in our school."

He was right. Since joining the yearbook, I had learned to my horror that people I'd known on a first-name basis had last names like Xarvoulakis, Wojcechowsky, Orailoglu, and Nwogalanya.

Mr. Brophy was good, but not that good.

Under his breath, to the tune of the Mickey Mouse Club theme song, John Christopher started singing: "X-A-R, V-O-U, L-A-K-I-S . . ."

"Ah, John, your mnemonic system rivals your glossal coordination," Mr. DeWaart said drily.

Rachel burst out laughing.

"What'd he say?" John asked.

"Your memory's as good as your tongue control," Rachel informed him.

"So I can count on you to go, Mr. Christopher?" Mr. DeWaart went on.

"Uh-uh, not tonight," John said. "I have to take care of my little bro while my 'rents go out."

Liz, Rachel, and Rosie all chimed in with excuses.

Finally Mr. DeWaart turned to Ariana. "What do you say, editor in chief?"

Ariana looked as if she wanted to say yes, but I could see Smut squeezing her hand.

"Um, I did have plans," she said, "but I guess . . ."

Her voice trailed off. I couldn't believe everyone was chickening out. And, Smut — he was trying to *force* Ariana not to do it. I thought they were all selfish, lazy jerks.

"I'll do it," I said.

And that was how I became Ariana's knight in shining armor. And why I was curious about Ariana's whereabouts after the party. And how I ended up in the Ramble with a human Gumby.

Fast-forward to that night. In the shower, rewinding that party in my mind, wondering why I'd been so curious about Ariana and Smut. Why I couldn't have walked to the print shop the regular way. Not to mention the yearbook. It was still sitting there, unproofed, because I was off having the worst night of my life.

My skin began shriveling, and I turned the water off.

In the bathroom's misty silence, questions continued to pound me: What next? Should I call the police? How would I explain the body to them?

If I were a cop, who would I suspect?

Me. I was the only person at the scene. I had no weapon, but I could have ditched it somewhere. At the very least, I'd have to explain what I was doing in the Ramble.

I could see the headlines now. Seventeen-year-old Peeping Tom from Nice Family Caught in Bizarre Killing. The TV news would show cops escorting me up the courthouse steps in handcuffs with a windbreaker over my head. Neighbors would insist I was a good kid, a gifted boy, but with a suspicious quiet streak.

As I slipped upstairs to my bedroom, I could hear Mom coming out her bedroom door. "David — ?"

"I'm beat, Mom. See you in the morning, okay?"

I heard her exasperated sigh. I plopped on my bed, looking up into the blackness. All I could see was the face. The hollow, spongelike person who'd been left to die. He'd come home with me and wasn't going to leave me alone.

I jumped out of bed and felt my way across the room to my closet. Pulling the door open, I flicked on the overhead light. Years ago, after my dad died, I became scared of just about everything. I turned on that light every night for months. It had made me feel safer then, and it did now.

Still, I had terrible insomnia. But I know I must have slept. Because that night I had yet another bizarre dream.

PART TWO

Mark

Chapter 6

". . . *ghoulish story . . . bodies discovered side by side . . . possible double suicide . . . both sought cures for neurological disease . . . retired police chief . . . cannot explain disappearance . . . police incompetence . . . county-wide search . . . possible vandalism. . . .*"

Marky hears the words in his sleep.

They are grown-up words but he understands some of them yes he does because he is a smart boy a gifted boy Miss Cramer his kindergarten teacher said so.

VANDALISM is what some kids did to the car and INCOMPETENCE is what the checkout people have at the A&P, plus he's heard of NEUROLOGICAL, which has something to do with Mommy and Daddy's sickness and

Mommy and Daddy have the TV turned up too loud.

But no, silly Marky, Yiayia is downstairs, sheesh don't you remember? Mommy and Daddy are at the faraway doctor's in New York for treatment. Oh and YIAYIA is a Greek word he knows, too, which means grandmother. He can call her that even though she's American Greek and not Greek Greek.

And he knows POSSIBLE and GHOULISH (Mommy Daddy) and SUICIDE and (Mommy Daddy!) and DISAPPEARANCE and

"Yiayia!"

Marky wakes up with a scream. The TV is blasting in the den downstairs, and Yiayia is crying. Much worse than the time she got a phone call from Greece when her mommy died. It sounds like she is watching the news, which he hates, and besides it's TOO LOUD. He gets out of bed, even though he is not supposed to after bedtime. But this is an EMERGENCY so Mommy and Daddy would say it was all right. Yiayia could call them in New York to ask them if she wanted.

"Yiayia?"

She doesn't hear him. Her cries sound like big gulps now. Marky feels nervous. He walks into the den and sees Yiayia doing her cross. Her shoulders are shuddering up and down. On TV he can make out a familiar-looking office building. It looks like the place where Daddy and Mommy work. Then Yiayia turns to him. Her eyes are red and wet and scary. She says his name and holds out her arms to him.

Marky wants to turn and run. He knows what has happened. But his body cannot move. Instead, he bends over and gets sick right there on the den carpet.

PART THREE

David

Chapter 7

"No!"

I sat upright in bed. The closet light was still burning. Outside my bedroom window a bird skittered by, looking almost liquid in the silver-gray morning light.

My body felt clenched up, my legs ached where they'd been cut. The dream was fading, but pieces of it still clung to a cobwebby corner of my brain. I shook my head, as if I could fling the dream away like droplets of water after a shower. I was actually shivering with fear. But why? I didn't *know* the people in the dream. Did I?

Marky.

Who was *Marky*?

Mark Rosenthal? As a kid? Impossible. For one thing, his grandmother is Jewish, not Greek.

Maybe the kid was me. I sure felt close to

him, and I do call my grandmother Yiayia. But she's in Greece, and nothing else in the dream happened in my life. It wasn't even my house. Nothing looked right. The TV was kind of a strange, long shape, and the clothes were some ugly style I'd never seen.

Hmm, maybe Marky was an alien.

The dream fragments were breaking up now, like a radio station in a car speeding too far from the signal. Last night's reality shoved itself back into my mind.

Or was Gumby a dream, too? I hoped so. Desperately.

"Are you okay in there?"

My mom was outside my door. Her voice was thick with early morning grogginess.

"Fine," I replied.

She took that as an invitation to come in. In her robe, flannel nightgown, and bare feet, she seemed small and fragile. She hardly ever looks that way, and it was kind of refreshing. "Hi, sweetie. You had a nightmare, huh?"

"I guess." I plopped my head back on my pillow, trying to look as if I needed to go back to sleep.

The truth? I was wide awake and flying.

"David . . ."

My mom has about seven hundred ways of

saying my name. This was Number 359: the *suspicious* "David."

"Your pants in the sink? They're full of mud and grass."

This threw me a little, because I thought she'd been upstairs sleeping the whole night. "Oh, sorry," I said.

"You had a little *outdoor* proofreading?"

"Mom . . . I'm tired. . . . It's Saturday."

She let out a sigh and stood up. "Look, David, I know you're not a boy anymore. But as long as you live in my house, you follow my rules. One: Come home when we agree, or call if you're going to be late. Two: Don't do anything . . . *foolish* you cannot take a man's responsibility for."

A man's responsibility! Suddenly, in her mind, I'd turned into every mom's nightmare. My Son the Stud. I wanted to burst out laughing and say, "Thanks for the compliment!" I didn't know who was the worse wishful thinker, her or me.

"I didn't, Mom," I said. "Don't worry."

"All right . . . if you say so."

As she shuffled back out of my room, I couldn't stop myself from blurting out, "Mom!"

She turned around. "Uh-huh?"

No.

I couldn't tell her. It was too gruesome. She'd get hysterical. She'd call the cops. The school. The FBI. And what if I *had* dreamed the whole thing?

"Nothing," I said.

She gave me a weird glance and left. I caught a glimpse of my digital clock: 5:28.

I got dressed quietly. No way was I going to sleep. I also had no intention of sitting there thinking about Gumby. I had to get my mind off it . . . *him*.

No one had proofread the yearbook the night before, but Mr. Brophy had told Mr. DeWaart it could be done early this morning. I didn't know what time Someday My Prints Will Come was open, but I'd find out.

And I would take the overland route to get there, as far from the Ramble as I could go.

"Aaagh! Someone hold me up! I'm seeing things!" Mr. Brophy said, clutching his heart and staggering backward on the print shop's front steps. His gray, shoulder-length, aging-hippie hair fell across his pasty face.

He was joking, I assumed. But on this particular day, that particular kind of joke made me nervous. I smiled to humor him.

"It's . . . it's *a high school senior awake before noon on a Saturday!*" he gasped.

"Hey, some of us have to work hard," I managed.

Mr. Brophy put his key in the front door. "Yeah, to make up for the other slobs, huh? Come on in. I have the mechanicals laid out for you. The photos aren't pasted down yet, but you've got them marked on the back, right?"

"Right."

"Matching pictures to names is something I can do pretty well," he said. "It's the names themselves that get me. My eyes cross after six letters."

I followed him in, feeling queasy, thinking about what lay in the river a few hundred yards away. I vowed not to say a thing about it. If Gumby was a dream, I'd forget it eventually. If he was real, *somebody* would discover him. There would be an explanation, and I'd be able to forget the whole thing.

I went through the motions of proofreading. I vaguely remember correcting a few last names and skimming over some quotes, poems, and captions. But my concentration was shot. The letters on each page seemed to swarm like ants. Under the circumstances, I did the best I could do.

On my way out, I saw Mr. Brophy racing around the shop. Employees were straggling in, and machines were whirring. "Thursday okay?" he shouted.

"*This* Thursday?" I asked. "To print them *and* bind them?"

"What do you think I run here? A bunch of Benedictine monks with quills? I do everything in-house — and you guys ain't the only school I'm doing. I'm like an accountant at tax time. I need to get you out of the way for the crunch, that's all."

"Thursday would be great," I said.

He rummaged around a pile of papers and pulled out an envelope small enough to hold a yearbook photo. "This is the weird shot. You want one copy for each absentee, right?"

"Yep," I said.

Mr. Brophy gave me a sly half-grin and shook his head. "You guys are sick, man. Worse than we were at your age."

"They had photographs back then?"

"Out!" Mr. Brophy picked up an X-Acto knife and held it like a dagger. "Out, brazen child!"

I ran from the shop, surprised I had any sense of humor left.

Over the weekend, no one said a thing about a body. I listened to the local news each evening and kept my ears open in town.

On Monday morning, as I approached Wetherby High, I noticed three police cars parked in front.

Inside the lobby, students were gathered near the office doors of our principal, Mr. Dutton. I could see Ariana, Smut, and a friend of theirs named Monique Flores.

Monique is blond, wispy, smart, and very emotional. (When she found out she was class salutatorian, she burst into tears of disappointment.) Ariana and Smut were on either side of her, arm in arm, as if they had to support her.

"What happened?" I asked them.

"Rick Arnold's . . . *missing*," Monique said gravely, between sniffles. "The police are talking to Mr. Dutton about it."

"His parents are in there," Ariana added. "They're hysterical."

"Wow," I replied. "When did they notice he was missing?"

"They've been looking since the weekend," Smut said. "But they didn't want to make a big deal about it. You know Rick. They figured he hitched down to Vanderbilt to camp out at his brother's college dorm. He does that sometimes."

"And he didn't?" I asked.

Smut shook his head. "They'd have known

by now. They think either he hitched with some wacko kidnapper, or he's hiding out around here."

"Did they mention anything about him, like what he was wearing?" I asked.

Ariana looked me in the eye. "Black shirt and black pants. Why?"

That confirmed it. I pictured the face in the Ramble and mentally filled it in with a skull and some cheekbones.

Gumby was Rick Arnold.

And I was the only one who knew where he was.

The door to the principal's office swung open, and a stocky, youngish policeman stepped out.

"Uh, please disperse," he shouted. "Come on, let's decongest the egress." (I never have understood why cops talk like that. This guy sounded like a taxidermist who took a wrong turn.)

I looked beyond him and caught a glimpse of Mr. and Mrs. Arnold inside the office, their faces streaked with tears.

I couldn't hold it in any longer. I stepped forward, staring at the policeman. He looked at me as if I were approaching the President of the United States with explosives strapped to my body.

"Move along, pal," he said with a steely glare. "Ain't you got homeroom?" His fingers instinctively perched near his billy club.

That I understood. I froze in my tracks as he disappeared back into the office.

Chapter 8

Whack!

The door to the yearbook office, heavy and wooden and stained with decades of student fingerprints, slammed shut.

I'd thought I was alone. I was sitting at Mr. DeWaart's long desk, trying to calm my jitters. Even though the yearbook was finished, the desk was still piled so high with papers, a sneeze would bury anyone within five feet of it. At that point I found it the most comforting, private place in the school.

Until I looked up and saw Ariana.

She was staring at me with a mixture of annoyance, suspicion, and rage.

In a moment, my mind flashed with a ridiculous idea. She and Smut had killed Rick.

"So . . ." My voice was like sandpaper. I had to swallow before going on. "Three more days till the shipment, huh? Do you think Mr. Brophy will come through — "

"You *know* something," Ariana interrupted.

I stared at her, slack-jawed.

"Come on, David, you can't lie to me. You really had no idea Rick was missing until this morning?"

"No! I found out from you, remember?" I lied beautifully. If we were in a movie, I'd have won an Academy Award.

"Then why was your first question 'How long was he missing?'? And why did you turn the color of plaster when I mentioned the clothes he was wearing?"

"Did I? Clothes? I don't remember that. . . ."

Whoops, forget it. My Oscar was flying out the window.

"Talk, David. And talk fast. First period begins in five minutes, and you never know who's going to pop in here for a morning chat."

I took a deep breath. I had to tell someone.

"Okay," I said. "But I think you should sit down."

Ariana's eyes didn't waver from me as I slowly told her everything. (Well, everything except the part about the Chevy with the steamy windows.)

By the time I finished, she was grimacing as if she'd just bit into a hunk of moldy bread. "This isn't like some late April Fool's thing, is it?"

"I wish, Ariana."

She let out a breath and buried her face in her hands. "If you're telling the truth, David, you're a coward. If you're not, you're a nut case. I'm not sure which one I believe."

"I'm not a nut case."

"And I'm not a coward," she replied, looking up. "If you don't go straight to the police, I will."

Her eyes were firm and frosty. "Don't," I said softly. "I'll go."

Ariana stood up and headed for the door. "Good luck, David."

After a moment I went into the hallway. The police had left Mr. Dutton's office, but they were gathered by their cars outside. I recognized Chief Hayes, a tall, gray-haired black man solemnly barking orders to a younger cop.

"Chief Hayes!" I called, stepping out the door.

" 'S'my name," he mumbled over his shoulder.

"I — I can show you where Rick Arnold is."

He turned to face me, with what might have

been a tic of interest in his stony expression. "Get in my car."

I obeyed. He did some last-minute ordering around, then climbed into the driver's seat. "What's your name, kid," he said, starting up, "and where are we going?"

"David Kallas," I replied. "And . . . the Ramble, near Cass and River View."

Chief Hayes's face remained unmoved. But his hand yanked the automatic shift straight past Drive and all the way to L2. Murmuring a curse, he flicked it back up again. "You . . . saw the missing person in the Ramble, son?"

"Yes."

"Am I correct in assuming, since you say this person is still there, that he is not presently alive?"

I felt absurdly guilty. I think if he'd asked me to confess to the murder, I'd have done it. "Yes."

The car screeched away from the curb as he said something under his breath. I believe it was "Lord, have mercy."

I was seized with violent chills as Chief Hayes parked by the Ramble. He noticed right away.

"You don't have to come with me, you know," he said. "As long as you give me the location of the body."

"Okay," I replied, but I was shaking so badly, it came out more like *Kuh*. "T-to the left of — of the car p-path."

"Near the big drainpipe?" he asked.

I nodded.

"Stay here. Take deep breaths and put your head between your knees. If you feel sick, for God's sake, get out of the car."

Chief Hayes wasn't going to win points for sensitivity.

I watched him plod into the woods. I figured he must have been about sixty, but he was still a bull of a man. He had a slight limp, which somehow made him look tough and heroic.

Chief Hayes was gone about a half-hour, I think. When he came back, he looked as if he'd aged ten years. His taut, wary features had gone droopy like a basset hound's, and his eyes were glassy.

Neither of us said a word as he plopped into the front seat. He stared at a spot just above the steering wheel.

"I — I didn't do it," I said weakly.

Chief Hayes nodded. "I know." He took his radio mike from its holder and put it slowly to his mouth. "Sergeant Kinsman, do you read me?"

"Yeah, Chief," a voice crackled back.

"We have located a male corpse matching the description of the Arnold boy."

As he gave the details in a dull monotone, he rubbed the back of his left hand against his eyes. I noticed a wet sheen along his thumb when he pulled his hand away.

If I didn't think such a thing was impossible, I'd be convinced Chief Hayes was crying. He slammed the mike down after he was done and muttered something about hay fever.

Another cop car arrived in minutes. Chief Hayes went out for a conference, then came back in and started the car.

He pulled away from the curb jerkily and nearly rammed into a road construction site barrier. Then he ran a stop sign on Cass, only to slam on the brakes and curse. I'd have offered to drive, but I was afraid he'd throw me in jail for asking. Instead, I settled back and was thankful we weren't in a high-speed chase.

Eventually we arrived at the police headquarters, a squat, yellow-brick building in the same Late Eyesore style as the rest of downtown Wetherby. Chief Hayes led me inside. His office was at the end of a dim, tiled hall.

Inside, a rotating fan swept past file folders stacked on a row of metal cabinets. Jutting triangular corners of paper razzed us like small white tongues in the breeze. Chief Hayes sat behind a wooden desk covered with papers and an old computer. I sank into the torn green cushion of a chair opposite him. I noticed a chunk of wood was missing from the lip of his desk on my side, about the size and shape of a bite mark. I couldn't imagine what jail must be like if *this* was the police chief's office.

Chief Hayes lit up a cigarette and pulled a clean ashtray out of a drawer. Then he asked a few basic *who, what, when, where, why* questions. But he didn't ask me about the sunken face or the hollowed-out body. I figured he mustn't have noticed. After a few days in the warmish weather, surrounded by animals, the body must have been in an advanced stage of . . . well, not *whole* enough to seem unusual.

I counted the butts that piled up in his ashtray and lost track at seven. The fan was useless against the thick smoke. My eyes stung, and I began coughing.

"Sorry, bud." Chief Hayes stood up, stubbing out his cigarette, and started opening windows. "I don't normally smoke — quit four years ago."

"It's okay," I rasped.

"In case you're wondering," he added, sitting back down, "I don't normally run stop signs, either."

Or cry, I wanted to say.

"Over forty years in the force," he said, "and it's still hard to see something like that."

I nodded.

He fiddled with his pen, deep in thought, then pointed to an old framed photo on the wall. "Go over and take a good look at that."

I did. It was a group portrait of a Wetherby High School basketball team, the paper yellowed with age and drooping. In the center stood a young, much rounder Chief Hayes. Next to him was the only smiling person on the team, a skinny black kid who towered over all the rest. His arm was resting comfortably on Chief Hayes's shoulder.

"Notice how many boys of color on that team?" he asked.

"Two," I said.

"Me and Reggie Borden. I wasn't much of a player, but Reggie was six five, a hundred thirty, and had a mean jump shot. Also a mouth like an outboard motor, and a mind like a trap. Funny, too. He used to say that jokes were his ammunition. Couldn't decide whether to be a philosopher, professor, or doctor. Or all.

Around here, in the forties and fifties, black people didn't think in those terms. Even though some of our families had been here for generations."

"The Underground Railroad," I said.

Chief Hayes smiled. "You've been doing your Jonas Lyte homework. Well, Reggie was headed for college, and kids were jealous of him — white and black. Our school had what we called 'secret societies' back then — high-toned frats, really. A couple were racist gangs, and they *really* hated Reggie. Me, I was a terrible student, and I didn't feel worthy of him — like maybe he was my buddy *only* because of my skin color. I found out I was wrong. . . ." His voice drifted off.

I couldn't believe Chief Hayes was telling me all this. A minute ago I'd have been grateful for a brief exchange about the weather. "What happened to him?" I asked.

Chief Hayes rose and stared out the window. "One day Reggie didn't show up at school. His parents didn't know where he was. After a week, the police — all white, of course — conducted a search, when they could be drawn away from their busy schedule of parking tickets. After another week, they concluded he'd run away from home. End of case. Well, some people figured Reggie was kidnapped by one of those racist groups. A lawyer tried to bring a suit, but it was dropped for lack of evidence. I was angry. I decided then and there I would be a cop someday. And that was when I realized how Reggie had influenced me. Before I met him, my idea of the future was tomorrow morning. He'd have been proud. . . ."

Chief Hayes had to clear his throat before going on. "Anyway, three other students were reported missing right afterward — and they were all white. The weird thing is, those kids were found."

"Alive?"

"Dead. Their bodies were disintegrating by the drainpipe in the Ramble."

I felt a shiver. A question popped to mind. "Chief Hayes, when did this all happen?"

Chief Hayes turned from the window and looked me in the eye for the first time. "Spring of 1950, David. Right after the earthquake."

Chapter 9

Chief Hayes drove me back to school. Afterward, I went straight to the library to ask Mrs. Klatsch a few things.

"Reggie who?" was her response to my first question.

I leaned over her desk and repeated, "Borden. He was a senior in 1950 — basketball star, African-American . . ."

"The fellow who disappeared! Yes, of course." Mrs. Klatsch raised a wary eyebrow. "Don't tell me you want to play sleuth, David. You know, Pudgy Hayes was his best friend, and he spent years looking into it."

"Pudgy?"

"Charles Hayes. He's now the police chief."

I loved it. Chief Pudgy. Officer Pudge. The blackmail potential was fantastic. "Uh, what did he find?"

"Just rumors: Reggie was a small-time convict in Seattle, a beggar in Chicago. . . . All nonsense, of course. I'd be less surprised if he were a college professor or a company president — even a movie star." She chuckled and stood up from her desk. "Well, you're welcome to try to find what no one else has, David. I'll get you microfilms of the 1950 newspapers. We may have a copy of that year's *Voyager* in the Local History section."

I was determined to find out about Reggie Borden and his disappearance. Were the events of 1950 connected to this year's? How could they be? A kidnapper or murderer from back then might be pushing a walker now.

Still, you never knew.

I found the yearbook and looked through it. Under Reggie's senior photo was the name REGINALD PHILIP BORDEN III and a long list of activities. In the book's front section I found the same basketball team photo that had been hanging on Chief Pudgy's wall. Reggie was also in photos of the Glee Club, the Key Club, the Honor Society, the Prom Committee, and the "Masque and Wig." That last one, which was the drama club, had a two-page spread. The play that year was an Agatha Christie mystery, and one photo showed Reggie emerging from a trick bookcase that turned on a central pivot.

The book was noncirculating, so I photocopied everything I needed. Then, when Mrs. Klatsch came back with two spools of microfilm, I buried my face in the machine and read until I was bleary-eyed. I made these copies, from the two newspapers:

(*Boston Globe*, February 8)

Tremor Rocks
Unsuspecting Village

A minor quake topped trees, set a major fire, and rattled nerves in Wetherby, a sleepy village known primarily for its witch trials of three centuries ago. . . .

(*Wetherby Herald*, February 12)

News and Views
From the Publisher

by Marvin Routledge

In the wake of Friday's tremor, I have heard residents call our village "cursed." Though others judge us harshly by our history, we residents must celebrate our uniqueness.

A quake in New England can be a source of public relations and pride! Yes, our fault can be our virtue!

(Same issue, Letter to the Editor)

Dear Sirs:

We must not ignore the menace in our own backyard! I am flabbergasted at those who accept the preposterous idea that an earthquake occurred in Wetherby, when there is ample proof of a secret underground Communist stronghold, assembling and testing nuclear weapons. . . .

(*Wetherby Herald*, February 20)

Red Menace Among Our Youth?

The County Bureau of Investigation today announced findings of a covert organization recruiting juvenile members. This group, believed to be led by outside Communist agitators, held meetings in the Wetherby High School basement, which has been sealed until further notice.

(*Wetherby Herald*, April 20)

High School Student Missing

A 17-year-old Negro boy, Reginald P. Borden, has been reported missing for four days. Reginald, a WHS senior, is 6 feet 3 inches tall and 132 pounds and has been active in sports and dramatics. Wetherby police are seeking clues.

(*Boston Globe*, April 23)

Remains Found in Western Mass. Town

Yesterday, in a wooded area bordering Wetherby, Mass., a hiker discovered clothing fragments and human remains, later identified as belonging to three missing high school students: Walter Dusenberg, Maria

Perez, and Benjamin Forsythe. A classmate of theirs, Reginald Borden, also missing, is being sought as a possible murder suspect. . . .

(*Wetherby Herald*, April 25)

Links Sought
In Ramble Tragedy

Wetherby police are investigating possible clues linking the disappearance of Reginald Borden, the tragic deaths of three high school students, and a recently uncovered organization thought to be subversive. . . .

(*Wetherby Herald*, November 19)

Tremor Source Studied

Following a study by the Army Corps of Engineers, which suggested an underground testing of explosives could have set off last winter's tremor, a team of geologic experts has discovered what appears to be a collapsed

limestone vault approximately
forty feet under the town common. . . .

(*Wetherby Herald*, December 6)

Fertilize That Soil!

It's true. The mineral content
of our soil has suffered greatly
this year. Levels of iron, potas-
sium, and especially calcium are
historically low. Why? Perhaps
the postwar boom is taxing our
resources. But whatever the
reason, be sure to stock up on
fertilizer at the Farrell Nur-
sery. . . .

I didn't know where all this stuff was going
to lead, but I knew it would lead somewhere.

I kept copies of the clippings, thanked Mrs.
Klatsch, and went home to think.

Chapter 10

Rick was dead. The news hit WHS like a sledgehammer. Classes were cancelled on Tuesday. The hallways rang with sobbing on Wednesday. We had "grief seminars" with the school psychologist, plus an assembly about safety. I'd never seen so many parents picking up their kids after school. *No one* went out at night.

Chief Hayes had left me out of the official report — for my own safety, he said. Ariana grilled me about my visit with him, but she agreed to keep it a secret.

I felt miserable. My secret festered inside me, until I felt like screaming the truth. I didn't know how I'd make it through the week.

On Thursday morning, an old VW van full of yearbook cartons pulled up to the school. Right on schedule. At least Mr. Brophy hadn't been affected by the murder.

As I carried a carton into the office, a senior named Jason Herman ran up alongside of me. His smile was the first I'd seen in a while.

"Is this it?" Jason asked. "*The* day?"

"Yep," I replied, placing the carton on the office floor. "And you're the first customer. Are you paid up?"

"I think. I forgot."

"Excuse me!" Ariana chimed in as she, John, Rosie, and Rachel barged by me carrying boxes.

A moment later Ariana and Smut ran back out. "I'll get the last box," Ariana told him. "You get the hand trucks."

They split. (Smut is *so* obedient.)

From Mr. DeWaart's desk, I grabbed our computer printout of the senior class. I riffled through and read:

ALPHA. #	NAME	PD?
42	HAZEN, JESSICA	——
43	HEALD, ROBERT	CASH
44	HERMAN, JASON	CK

"Paid by check." I grabbed a box, ripped it open, and pulled out a yearbook. "You're all set. Enjoy."

"All *right*!" Jason walked away, leafing through the book.

"Is he gone?" John whispered, peeking out of the yearbook office.

"Yeah," I replied. "Why?"

"If I hear him complain one more time about how he got rejected from every college because they're not looking for psych majors — "

"He got wait-listed at one place," Rachel called from inside the office.

"Hallelujah," Rosie cheered.

Ariana came back in with the last box. "I just saw Jason with a book," she said.

"Yeah, he's paid," I replied.

She dropped the box inside the office. "You're not supposed to give them out individually. Each box goes to a specific homeroom. There's a list of paid-up kids inside each one."

"Oops — "

"Do something *right* for a change, okay?"

"I — I didn't know, all right?"

"Hey, whoa, chill out," John said. "We're all a little upset, but we have to stay cool with each other. . . ."

Ariana sighed. "Yeah. Sorry, David — "

Smut came roaring into the lobby, wheeling two hand trucks. "Load 'em up! We've got about eight minutes."

We stacked boxes on the trucks and quickly

rolled them into the hallways. The six of us were able to distribute the books quickly to the eight senior homerooms.

When we got back, Jason was waiting.

He did not look happy.

"What's the idea?" he said, holding the book open to us.

Jason, in case you hadn't guessed, had missed the yearbook photo shoot, which meant he'd become a Bananahead.

"You asked for it, David," Ariana murmured.

"Jason," I said with my smoothest nice-guy smile, "it was only meant as a joke. . . ."

"A *joke?* Putting this . . . *thing* over my name?"

I held my breath to avoid laughing, which would have really upset Jason. Then I glanced where he was pointing.

The Bananahead was nowhere to be seen.

Above Jason's name was a black-and-white photo of a shrunken human face. It was festooned with dried flesh, and blood dripped from its mouth.

My jaw fell open. It looked like Rick — or what was left of him in the Ramble.

Behind me, Ariana sucked in air. Smut said, "How did that get there?"

"I have my ideas," Jason slammed the book shut and gave him an angry smirk. "Subconscious hostility toward me . . . repressed envy . . . maybe whoever did this had inadequate love as a child. But you know what? I don't care. You give me my money back. My mom's a lawyer, you know, and you can expect to hear from her."

"Just a minute." Feeling numb, I walked into the *Voyager* office. Mr. DeWaart was sitting at his desk, staring at an open yearbook.

"Hi," I said. "Uh, Jason wants his money back."

"And he'll get it," Mr. DeWaart snapped.

"Thank you," Jason said from behind me. He ceremoniously dropped the yearbook onto the floor. It made a loud *whomp,* and he marched off.

I picked it up, then huddled inside the office with Ariana, Smut, Rosie, John, and Rachel. Mr. DeWaart shut the door and glared at me. "You did proofread this, no?"

"Yes, but — "

Ariana cut me off. "Was this one of your crazy ideas, David? I mean, if you have something against Jason, this was a stupid way to express it!"

Before I could reply, Mr. DeWaart shoved

the book toward us and said, "It wasn't just Jason."

Ariana took it. We all looked over her shoulder as she flipped through. The shrunken head was all over the place — above every single name that was supposed to have had a Bananahead over it.

"I've never seen this picture before!" I insisted. "We gave Mr. Brophy the Bananahead shot, remember? Rosie put it in a small envelope. When I got to the printer that Saturday, the photos hadn't been pasted down yet. But Mr. Brophy had the envelope. He held it up and asked me about it before I left the printer. He made a joke about it."

"Did you actually see what was in the envelope?" Mr. DeWaart asked.

"No . . ."

"Hey, before you guys get any funny ideas, let me just say for the record that I did *not* switch those photos," Rosie said.

"It must have been Brophy," Rachel concluded.

John nodded. "Figures. He fried his brain on LSD in the sixties. That stuff can have long-term effects, you know."

"Unfortunately, I'm the one who's going to have to cover for this." Mr. DeWaart sighed and looked at his watch. "Let me go to the office and make a P.A. announcement before the whole senior class descends on us with torches and pitchforks."

"Wait," Rachel said. "What are we going to do, take all the books back?"

"You bet," Mr. DeWaart replied, "for a full refund or a corrected printing of the book."

"But is that in the budget?" Ariana asked.

"No. But if Mr. Brophy is at fault, he'll pay for it."

"And if he's not?" Rosie said.

Mr. DeWaart shrugged. "I'll pay. It's my responsibility to produce an official yearbook."

Ariana and Smut followed him into the hallway, arguing. John and Rachel went off arguing about something else. Liz split with Rosie, who was still looking worried.

I sank into a chair with the yearbook. I leafed through, looking at that hideous face, time and time again.

Who could have done it? I wouldn't put it past Mr. Brophy, who *was* nuts. But he was also a businessman, and sabotaging a job was a good way to lose clients. Unless he did it by accident. For that matter, Rosie could have done it by accident, too — but would either of those two actually *own* a photo like that?

And just happen to have it hanging around in the wrong place at the wrong time?

Mr. DeWaart was the one who took the photo to the printer. He could have switched it. But why? He was the one offering to pay for a reprint.

It didn't make any sense.

I checked a few other parts of the book. The yearbook staff photo looked great, as did my "Then-and-Now" feature.

My own photo was ugly as usual. Underneath, my many activities were spelled out in great detail:

VOYAGER STAFF, 4.

Ariana's photo was every bit as sexy as she was. And her activity list took five lines of small type.

I turned to Rick Arnold's photo. Fortunately he'd shown up for the shoot. A shrunken head over *his* name would have been pretty disgusting. My heart tugged when I saw the bright, optimistic, friendly look on his face.

Then I read what was underneath:

CHOIR, 3; SPANISH CLUB, 1, 4; PROM
COMMITTEE.

Which "Most Likely" goes to Rick?
He isn't smart or cool or quick
Or careful, so perhaps that's why
He's likely, most of all, to die.

Chapter 11

I smelled it again.

That sick, sweet chalkiness I first smelled in the Ramble.

It seemed to float up from the book. The poem had brought it back.

That and the sense of something growing in my body. It was rumbling the walls of my stomach, speading like a cancer.

"Attention, seniors who have copies of the yearbook. You must return them. This is Mr. DeWaart and I will be in the yearbook office third period and after school. . . ."

As the announcement droned over the P.A. system, I took a deep breath. I tried to force away the memory of Rick Arnold's body.

The poem stared at me, colder and uglier than the shrunken-head photos. There had to be an explanation for it. Maybe Rick had had a sick sense of humor. Maybe he had known what was going to happen to him.

Maybe Mr. Brophy was psycho, bent on sabotaging our whole book.

Maybe nothing. It was my fault. I should have noticed the poem at the print shop and stopped it from being printed. Some proofing job I'd done. The state of mind I was in, I might as well have been proofing hieroglyph-ics. Anything could have gotten by me.

Anything.

With a sinking sensation, I wondered what else had.

I turned to the beginning of the photos and read every entry, beginning with Roy Abrams:

SENIOR CLASS RULES! YEAH!!!

And moving on to Anita Adamowsky:

It was great! Best of luck and love to all my friends. See ya in real life!

No wonder no one else had wanted to proof-read this stuff. It was boring.

It stayed that way, too, until I got to Laura Chase. She was one of the most popular girls in the class. Dumb as a brick, but popular. I

could not imagine her writing the poem I saw
under her name:

> *Pity, pity, Laura Chase,*
> *Pretty hair and pretty face,*
> *Isn't it a sorry fate*
> *She won't live to graduate?*

Not to mention the entry for Robert "Butthead" Heald, the All-State nose guard on our
football team whose highest academic achieve-
ment was recognizing the numbers on his opponents' jerseys:

> *Study? Not burly Bob Heald!*
> *'Cause his passion for football won't yield.*
> *So fold him in creases*
> *Then cut him to pieces*
> *And spread him all over the field.*

The next few dozen were normal, until Ed-
ward Lyman, whose picture was right before
Ariana's. Ed was quiet and antisocial and into
motorcycles, and his poem went like this:

> *Ed Lyman*
> *Hates rhymin'.*

See ya, Ed.
Dead.

And Janie Youmans, who'd had plastic sur-
gery to make herself look like the star of a
teen soap opera she loved, only to end up
hating the character:

> *Greetings to Janie P. Youmans*
> *Who fancies TV over humans*
> *Ask 'em, Jane, now while you're able,*
> *Will they wire your casket with cable?*

I was dizzy. I was sick. This couldn't be
happening. It was like some horrible, per-
verted *Spoon River Anthology.*
Rinnnnng!
I lurched in my chair. The yearbook fell to
the floor.
Easy, Kallas, I said to myself. It's only the
first-period bell.
I looked at the clock.
Okay, the *second*-period bell. I'd been so
buried in the yearbook, I hadn't noticed the
time go by.
I jammed one of the books into my backpack
and raced out of the office. The hallway was
filling up. Small groups were forming, all gath-

ered around copies of the yearbook. I could hear gasps. Murmurs. Bursts of laughter.

"Yo, Kallas!"

I turned to see Butthead Heald, holding a yearbook and bearing down on me as if I were the opposing quarterback. My life swam before my eyes.

He stopped before contact, sparing me instant pulverization. I stopped praying and prepared for an open-field run.

"Who did this?" he asked, looking down the winding pathway of his twice-broken nose. "You?"

"No," I squeaked.

His mouth edged upward, pushing aside the thick muscles of the rest of his face. "Well, whoever did it, it's great."

"Huh?"

"I laughed through first period, man," Butthead said. "It's like *National Lampoon* or *Spy*. Those funky old pictures . . . and the poem! Whoa! I found three of them — but mine was the best."

National Lampoon? Spy? I thought this guy gave up periodicals after *Ranger Rick*. "Uh, thanks."

"Hey, this'll be worth something someday, you know? See ya."

He sprinted way, carrying the yearbook like a football. And I felt grateful I was still in one piece.

I split pretty quickly; I didn't want to be around Butthead when he discovered Rick's poem. Even he wouldn't find that funny.

Only one other person liked the yearbook — Ed Lyman, who painted his own version of the shrunken head on the cover and refused to return it. As far as I could tell, the rest of the school was creeped out. I saw Janie Youmans in tears by her locker, surrounded by friends who were trying to comfort her. Laura Chase looked bone-white in English class.

After school we had an emergency *Voyager* staff meeting. Most of the yearbooks had been returned by then, and they were stacked by the door.

Mr. DeWaart looked even gloomier than usual. "I spoke to Jack Brophy," he said. "He says he pasted down the correct photos — and he did not personally set the text, so he couldn't have read any of the poems. However, he did offer to reprint the entire run *gratis,* and by the end of next week."

"I still say he did it," John remarked.

"John, we are no longer pointing fingers," Mr. DeWaart said. "Let's decide how to proceed."

We all pitched in with ideas. We decided to send an apology and a free book to the affected kids, and a copy of the sabotaged book to the police.

Just as we were discussing the future of the Bananahead shot, Mr. DeWaart decided to call the meeting.

"We'll continue this," he said, "but right now I've got promises to keep — "

" — and miles to go before I sleep," Smut cut in with a big smile.

A big, *teacher's pet* smile.

"Let us go then, you and I," Mr. DeWaart recited, gesturing to the hallway.

"Oh, gag me," Rachel groaned. "I'm allergic to Shakespeare, guys."

"Eliot," Smut said with a laugh. "And Frost."

He gave Mr. DeWaart a nauseating, smug look as the two of them walked away.

"I knew that was Eliot and Frost," John mumbled, watching them go.

Rosie shook his head with disgust. "I hate when they get like that. It's like a disease."

"Yeah," Ariana said. "Chronic Superiority

Complex. Stephen gets it before every Delphic Club meeting."

"I hate to say it, Ariana," Rachel grumbled, "but I'd smack that boyfriend if I were you."

"I've thought about it," Ariana replied.

"Invite me to see it," Rosie said. "I'll take pictures."

"We can charge admission!" Liz added. "And get Mr. Brophy to do posters."

"You *guys* . . ." Ariana's brow was uncreasing. A smile crept across her face.

We all started laughing. I guess I'd been wrong about Smut. Not everybody loved perfection.

"Well, I booketh," John said. "Comest thou, Juliet?"

"You bettest," Rachel replied, and they traipsed away into the hallway.

The rest of us left in a nice, normal exchange of good-byes.

I walked part of the way home with Ariana. I could tell she was sinking back into a funky mood. "Are you okay?" I asked.

"Yeah," she replied. "Why wouldn't I be?"

I shrugged. "Just asking. You look kind of bummed."

Ariana concentrated fiercely on the sidewalk for a few moments. Finally she said, "I . . . I feel weird saying this, but I'm jealous of Mr. DeWaart."

"Hey, you're just as smart as he is. He's just older."

"Yeah, but he's got Stephen." Ariana sighed.

"Why don't you join that club? I'm sure you qualify."

"Oh, please. The whole thing is so pretentious. *Delphic* means 'ambiguous,' at least according to Stephen. They think they're *so important* that they need to keep people guessing. Stephen says they discuss philosophy and politics and poetry and music. But I'm sure they just sit around nodding while Mr. DeWaart blows hot air. Of course, I'll never know for sure, because he's not supposed to talk about meetings. Even the meeting place is this big secret. Like anyone could care."

"Well, it sounds like you do care."

Ariana fell silent for a while. When she spoke again, her voice was subdued. "I guess I wouldn't mind so much if Monique Flores wasn't in the group."

"*She's* after S — Stephen?" (I almost said *Smut*, but Ariana hates that name.)

"Don't be fooled. Under that drippy exterior, she's incredibly ambitious. She wants him — and we all know she hates being second."

I listened. I gave support and advice. By the time we reached the turnoff to my street, I was the perfect friend and confidant.

But don't get me wrong, I was tap-dancing on the inside.

No one knew where The Delphic Club met. But I had an idea.

And if Smut *was* seeing Monique on the sly, Ariana would can him in a minute.

Chapter 12

I said good-bye to Ariana at the place where I usually veer off to go home.

I walked a block in the right direction, until she was out of sight. Then I broke into a sprint toward the high school.

When I got there, the front door was locked. I could see Mr. Sarro, our custodian, through the glass. He was pushing a broom across the lobby floor, holding his customary can of Coke in his free hand. I knocked loudly and got his attention.

He opened the door and said, "What's up, doc?"

"Some emergency yearbook work," I lied. "You heard about our problem?"

He nodded solemnly. "Say no more. Come on in."

Picking a key from the jangling arsenal attached to his belt, he let me into the office.

I thanked him, shut the door behind me, and stayed there listening to his off-key whistling in the hallway. When it faded away, I opened the door softly and bolted.

The backstage door was opposite a row of lockers around the corner from the office. I pulled it open and went inside.

In the dim light I saw tent flaps and circus props lying among brooms, wires, and empty paper cups. It all brought back fond memories of Smut as Billy Bigelow in *Carousel*, falling into the orchestra pit during a knife fight, then climbing back onstage after he was supposed to be dead.

It was a dramatic highlight of the year.

Across the stage I saw what looked like a round cage with an open gate. As I walked closer, I could see that the cage surrounded a spiral staircase leading into the basement.

My mind was racing faster than my feet. Chief Pudgy had talked about "secret societies" and "high-toned frats" in 1950. The newspaper clippings had mentioned "Communist agitators" meeting in the high school basement, which had to be "sealed off until further notice."

Nowadays the drama society had a scenery shop directly under the stage. I'd never been there, and I didn't know how big it was, but the school was sprawling and that meant the basement must be, too.

Plenty of room for a high-toned frat to meet.

A light shone from below. I went through the gate and descended into a large room crammed with all kinds of stuff I recognized from past plays.

The ratty sofa from *Arsenic and Old Lace*, the wheelchair from *The Man Who Came to Dinner*, the butter churn from *Oklahoma!*, the fake car from *Grease* — plus dressers, chairs, tables, chests, and mannequins. A bookcase lined one whole wall, and even that looked familiar.

Along another wall was a long, wooden workbench stocked with tools, supplies, and countless paint cans. Costume racks were jammed against a third wall.

The furniture, all different styles but all cheap-looking, had been arranged to create a kind of Living-Room-from-Hell effect against the fourth wall. It seemed like a perfect setting for a Delphic Club meeting.

I assumed they were still off rowing. (The Wampanoag River widens about three miles up the road in Baldwin Township, where the high school crew teams share a boathouse and have their meets and practices.) I also assumed they'd be back any minute. I had no time to hang out and enjoy the scenery.

I headed back upstairs. Had I found the great secret? I wished I could know.

Against the back wall of the stage I noticed a huge flat, covered with Day-Glo stars. It was left over from a corny scene in which Smut went to heaven. (Really, you had to see this play.) I hid behind it. If The Delphic Club didn't show up within ten minutes, I'd go back to the drawing board.

The first seven minutes were not pleasant. Mr. Sarro wandered onstage and sang "Memory" from *Cats* so loud and terribly, I almost barked. I stayed put until long after he left, just in case he decided to come back for an encore.

I was glad I did, because soon after I heard voices.

From the basement.

I couldn't believe it. Where had they been, hiding among the costumes?

The voices got louder, punctuated by clanging footsteps against the metal stairs. "I think Hamlet was a putz," one person said.

"A *putz*?" Mr. DeWaart repeated. "Hmmm, I like it . . . 'O what a putz and peasant slave am I. . . .'"

" 'In action how like an angel, in apprehension how like a putz!' " someone else said.

Laughter echoed across the stage. They

were walking toward the door to the hallway. One of them started humming, and they all joined in, harmonizing. I have to admit it sounded pretty good, especially after Mr. Sarro.

I took a step closer to the edge of the flat. I was angled so that I could see the group from behind.

Smut's arm was around Monique's shoulder. Yes! Yes!

There it was! Eyewitness proof! Smut being a two-timing jerk!

I felt resentment toward Monique, anger toward Smut, sympathy for Ariana.

But let's face it, many nice possibilities were opening up for me.

I had found out one thing Ariana wanted to know. Now I was determined to find another: The Delphic Club hiding place. Obviously the basement was larger than the scenery shop. I just had to find the entrance to the rest of it.

I ran toward the cage. Its gate was shut but not locked. The light no longer shone from below, and I didn't see a light switch, so I stepped downward into pitch darkness.

The stage light cast a pale circle onto the scenery shop floor. I went to the section of the wall I *could* see, then groped along it to the right, into darkness, carefully stepping over props and around furniture.

I came to the corner and went right. My fingers told me I'd reached the bookcase. No switch likely there. As I turned to go back, my foot hooked under something ankle-high.

I tumbled against the bookcase. Old, smelly classics rained down on me, one of which must have been an unabridged dictionary.

As I rubbed my poor aching head, I looked toward the stairs. From my low position I could now see a string hanging from the ceiling. I got up slowly, walked toward it, and pulled.

And there was light.

(I know. What a genius.)

Around me was the same ugly room I'd seen before. With several books missing from the bookcase. And a heavy barbell on the floor next to it.

My ankle was starting to throb, so I had to hobble around the room. I pushed aside the costume rack from the wall, but no door was behind it, and I got a mouthful of fake fur and a noseful of mothball stink.

I lifted a dusty old Oriental rug off the floor, hoping to see a trapdoor. Instead I saw a troupe of dust bunnies slam-dancing on linoleum tiles.

Some sleuth. For all I knew, The Delphic Club had beamed itself down from a spaceship into the basement, just to annoy me.

I limped over to the bookcase to replace the books I'd knocked down. As I bent to pick up the heaviest one, which happened to be *War and Peace* (ouch), I noticed that my fall had actually *moved* the bookcase. I could see where the bottom of the case had slid inward.

I had to stand on my toes to reach the shelf I had emptied.

"Aaagh!" I came down on my ankle too hard. My arm shot out toward the shelves to brace myself.

The bookcase moved again.

Great. One more time, I thought, and the whole thing would topple.

I bent to pick up another book, and then I froze.

I remembered where I had seen the bookcase before.

It was in a picture from the 1950 yearbook. Reggie Borden was emerging from behind it, in a stage set.

I dropped the book and leaned against the case firmly.

With a creak it swung away, into a vast, empty blackness.

Chapter 13

"Whoa . . ."

The space beyond the bookcase was huge.

It receded into darkness, the expanse broken by thick cement pillars. Rotting wood beams made rectangles in the ceiling, from which a few scraggly light bulbs hung.

I stepped inside, onto a floor of hard, welltrammeled dirt. The air was clammy and cold, and it smelled of mildew and dry rot.

I turned on two light bulbs. They swung jerkily as I let go, sending ghostly shimmers of light across the walls.

Plenty of students had found this place, besides The Delphic Club. Drawings and graffiti were all over the walls. This is what I saw on the nearest one:

BEANO + DELORES 1948
CLASS OF '73 RULES!!!

MAX YASGUR FOR PRESIDENT
IMPEACH NIXON!
TRAMPLE THE NAZI DOGS!
END IMPERIALISM! MARXISM NOW!
U.S. OUT OF VIETNAM
GEORGE LOVES CALI 4 EVER 1967

I stared at that last one. I felt my heart skip.

George and Cali are my parents.

Well, one is and one was.

The message stood out so proudly, as if it had been written yesterday. I could see Dad, seventeen and looking over his shoulder, not wanting to be caught.

4 Ever, it said. That was how long they expected to be in love. Forever.

They didn't make it. They had twenty years.

Twenty years seems so short. Yet the seven years since Dad died — *that* seems like forever. I guess it's because my time without him will never end.

Terrific. My eyes were watering. I hated thinking about Dad. I'd trained myself not to. It was too frustrating. Whenever I did, I always wanted to ask him questions — about sex, about Ariana, about this crazy yearbook stuff. I would picture him listening, but I couldn't picture his answer. Whenever I tried to imagine looking into his eyes, he was always looking back at a ten-year-old.

I needed to let my past alone. Reading about strangers was much easier.

Besides, some of the writing might answer what had actually happened down there in 1950.

A lot of the messages were faded or drawn over, but I could make out dates on quite a few. I saw plenty of writing from the forties, about Hitler and Mussolini and the atomic bomb. A couple of things were dated 1950, and lots of it was after 1965.

Absolutely nothing existed between those two dates.

The basement had been "sealed" after 1950, that much I remembered from the microfilm. But what exactly had happened down there?

I followed the writing deeper into the basement. Odd, unexpected corners opened into wider and wider areas, until the bookcase was nowhere to be seen.

The writing thinned out, then disappeared. But I didn't care. The air was sweeter here, and I was feeling light-headed.

At the end of the wall was a long, long crack in the dirt floor, which I followed with my eyes till it led to a wide opening fifteen feet away — through which a soft mist billowed and hissed.

I'm coming.

I breathed deeply and started to laugh. A hole in the earth, maybe that was where The Delphic Club met, an underground lair like the high-toned Communist-agitated frat.

Someone was giggling, cackling. It didn't shock me at all, and then I realized the laughing was *mine* and the smoke was circling my face and I was walking to the hole and I felt smart (*om . . . pha . . . los*) and powerful and charged with energy (Oh how weird what the hell did that mean?) and I never wanted to go back and I could live forever like that (4 Ever!) and behind me I could see the bookcase now and it was closing (Hamlet was a putz) and (Smut and Monique) and (what am I doing).

A strangled cry welled up from my toes. It exploded from my mouth, doubling and tripling off the walls.

I stood at the edge of the crack. My knees were locked, but I felt a piece of me ripping away, plunging in the blackness.

My heart was a jackhammer, my brain a tangle of loose sparking wires. Before the last echo of my cry faded, I turned and ran.

The bookcase was in view when I blacked out.

And another dream rushed in to fill the void.

PART FOUR

Mark

Chapter 14

"Marky, our company's here!"

Splursh. Spllllat!

"MARKY!" Yiayia screams from the living room.

The ketchup lands in little shiny clumps on the carpet. Marky steps in them.

He hears the front door open and some strange woman's voice squeal hello. Yiayia and she jabber on about how long it has been and how wonderful each other looks.

Marky opens his mouth, squirts some of the ketchup inside, and keeps it there without swallowing. For good measure, he gives his white T-shirt a blast, right over his heart.

Oh, and some in his hair, of course.

He hides the ketchup bottle under his bed. Then he lies down, his matted hair right in one of the red puddles on the carpet. Facing upward, he spits. The ketchup, thinned by his saliva, trickles down the sides of his mouth.

"MARKY! Just a sec, Joyce. He's probably got his headphones on. Eight years old and he can't go a minute without — "

The bedroom door swings open, and Yiayia swallows her last word. Marky wishes he could see the expression on her face, but that would mean opening his eyes.

Yiayia's scream is worth the trouble, even though it is the loudest scream he has ever heard and he thinks he has lost some hearing.

"Oh! Oh! Oh! Oh! Help!"

The gasps are great, too. Like hiccups.

Then she has to go spoil it by jumping on him. He doesn't expect that. Also he doesn't expect her to start pounding his chest.

Putting her lips on his is the last straw.

"Stop! Ew! Ew!" he cries.

Yiayia's eyes are enormous. Her mouth is ringed with ketchup, and curled into this gross shape, like a kidney bean.

Behind her, Joyce Somebody stands gaping in the doorway.

"You almost gave me a heart attack!" Yiayia shrieks. "Is this your idea of a joke?"

Marky bursts out laughing. Yiayia looks like a clown with that ketchup around her mouth.

"I want you and this room cleaned up, right now! And no dinner for you tonight!"

All riiiight! Marky thinks. He doesn't want to have dinner with those old farts anyway. All Yiayia ever likes to talk about is one thing.

She slams the door, and Marky hears footsteps receding down the hall.

"I'm so sorry, Joyce. He never used to be like this. His parents' death was huge trauma. I'm looking for a therapist right now for him. . . . "

There she goes. Starting already. Only this time he doesn't have to sit there and take it. His parents aren't dead. The bodies were never found. Dead bodies don't just walk away. Someday they are going to come back.

And then what will Yiayia do? She'll have nothing to talk about.

Which is just fine.

PART FIVE

David

Chapter 15

"David!"

I was fading into consciousness. My eyelids fluttered.

"David! Are you all right?"

It took a few seconds for Ariana's face to come into focus. She was leaning over me, still in a down coat. Her face was streaked with tears. Behind her the bookcase was ajar, and I could see into the scenery shop.

"Yeah," I groaned. "I — I just tripped, I guess. How did you find me?"

"Mr. Sarro told me you were in the office, but it was empty when we checked. Then he said he heard voices in the auditorium. I saw the gate open and the light on in the scenery shop, so — "

"Why did you come? I thought you went home."

"I was going to, but — but — "

Ariana's face crumpled. Tears began streaming down her cheeks.

I sat up and let her bury her head in my shoulders. "What? What happened?"

Her answer was a fit of moaning, keening cries. She couldn't speak. I gently helped her up, trying to keep weight off my bum ankle. As she sat on a sofa in the scenery shop, I swung the bookcase inward.

I took one last look into the basement cavern and saw the graffiti on the walls. I remembered reading some of it, but that was all. The rest was a blank.

But I did recall turning the lights on. And now they were off.

The bookcase slid into place, and I sank into the sofa. "Ariana," I asked, putting my arm around her, "did you shut the li — "

She clutched me so hard, it took away my breath. "Oh, David, it was horrible! Now I know how you felt. I — I — I don't know what — I — should we call the police? I want to move — I don't want to live here anymore — "

"You kids all right down there?" Mr. Sarro's voice boomed from above. "I mean, I don't want to interrupt, but I can't let you stay down there unsupervised, you know. Not that I don't trust you, but my job — "

I looked at Ariana. She wiped her eyes and nodded.

"No sweat, Mr. Sarro!" I said. "We're coming right up!"

I helped Ariana to her feet. As she climbed the spiral stairs, I pulled the light switch, then followed her up.

We went to the yearbook office, where I grabbed my coat. When we were finally outside, Ariana hugged me with both arms and began crying again.

Whoa.

If I could bottle how that felt, I'd keep it with me and take a sip every day for the rest of my life.

Had she found out about Smut and Monique? Was that what this was about? "What's wrong, Ariana?" I asked.

She swallowed hard. "Come with me."

As we walked arm in arm toward her house, my ankle began feeling stronger. Ariana was trembling, and I held her tightly.

We turned onto Cass. At the intersection with Eliot Place, we saw the construction site that Chief Pudgy had almost run into. Ariana stopped. Her face was practically white.

"L-l-look in there," she said. "I can't."

I left her on the corner and walked closer. Wooden sawhorses surrounded a gaping, rectangular hole in the road. Inside the hole was a corroded metal pipe that looked as if the Pilgrims had put it in themselves. The center had rotted away, and debris had collected inside it — newspapers, bottles, wrappers, a shoe. . . .

My eyes widened. I went to the edge and looked over.

The shoe had a foot in it. And it was attached to a leg.

"Oh my God," I said.

"What do we do?" Ariana asked.

"Is it real?"

"I don't know!"

As if in answer, the foot twitched.

Then, slowly, it slid into the pipe.

Chapter 16

We stopped running after three blocks. Clutching hands, we sat on a park bench along the Ramble.

For a long time we couldn't talk. Ariana rocked slowly back and forth, her eyes focused blankly on the sidewalk.

My head throbbed. The chalky smell was in my nostrils again. I sat forward, massaging my temples and breathing deeply.

Ariana finally turned to me, her eyes bloodshot and her teeth chattering. "What do we do now?"

"I don't . . . know." Each word was like a fist to the head. I gasped.

"David, are you okay?"

I nodded, then whispered, "I'll deal with it."

Ariana moved aside. "Lie down."

I did as she said. She looked down at me, her eyes now full of concern. "I'm sorry," she said with a sigh. "I've been so upset, I didn't even ask you about your accident."

"What accident?"

"Oh, my lord, amnesia." She began speaking slowly, as if to an infant. "I found you in the basement of Wetherby High School. Do you know where that is?"

"Well, yeah . . ."

"Good. Now, I think you may have a concussion, David. Do you have blurred vision?" She held up three fingers, like a Boy Scout salute. "How many fingers?"

I returned the salute. "On my honor, I will do my duty to God and country, and obey the Scout code . . ."

Ariana's face went blank. Then she scowled at me. "Very funny. You know, we have a serious situation here."

I was already feeling better, until I started to laugh, which was like inviting Arnold Schwarzenegger to sit on my head. "I don't have amnesia," I said, speaking slowly, "at least not completely. I went to the basement to look for The Delphic Club meeting place."

"You *what*?"

I told her everything I'd learned about Reggie Borden and the strange 1950 deaths. I described the rumors about the underground groups, and I told her my suspicions about The Delphic Club meeting in the basement.

Ariana listened closely, softly stroking my hair and nodding. "That feels so good," I said. "You have soft hands."

She laughed. "Soft hands? Stephen says my hands are like a truck driver's."

"He's lying. You could be a masseuse — or a painter or a pianist."

"*Please.* I'm much too practical. You need to be a dreamer for those things."

"You're not?"

"Uh-uh. Just the opposite. I discovered there was no Santa at the age of three, by stringing gum across the chimney. When the gum wasn't broken the next morning, I had my proof."

I sat up. "You *didn't*!"

Ariana nodded. "When I lost my first tooth I didn't put it under my pillow for the Tooth Fairy. I put it in a glass of Pepsi to see if it would decay."

"And . . . ?"

"It did. To a little pebble."

My pain was melting away — and so was the wall that had always been between Ariana and me. We were talking a lot, probably to avoid thinking about the Sewer Thing. But we were *one* now, united with a knowledge that no one else shared. And no matter what the outcome, we would carry this with us for the rest of our lives.

I smiled at her. Her eyes became moist. "Oh, David," she said, "what are we going to do?"

I didn't know whether she meant *do* about us or *do* about the foot in the sewer pipe.

But it didn't matter. I drew her close to me, and she didn't resist. I closed my eyes and gently opened my mouth.

The warmth of her kiss bathed me. The events of the past few days flew away, and I knew in my bones that Ariana and I belonged together.

When our lips parted, she rested her head on my chest. I felt so lucky. I wanted this to last.

But I started thinking about Smut.

"Uh, Ariana," I said, screwing up my courage. "When I was looking for the meeting place, I saw Stephen and Monique. You were right about them, you know. They were . . . well, kind of hanging all over each other."

Ariana stiffened. She let go of my hand and sank back into the bench. *"What?"*

"You know, arm in arm. . . . "

Ariana looked disgusted. "Is that what this was all about, David? You were just spying on Stephen? Trying to get me to like you?"

I tried putting my arm around her. "No! That's not it at all. I . . . I didn't mean to upset you."

She edged away. "I'm not upset," she said with a strange calmness. "Why should I be upset? I mean, classmates are dying, corpses are swimming in our water system, there's a hole under the school, our yearbook was sabotaged, you're busy checking out forty-year-old Communist conspiracies, and my boyfriend is seeing someone behind my back. What's the big deal?"

"Ariana — "

With a choked sob, she got up from the bench and ran toward her house. "Leave me alone."

I followed at a sprint. "I know how you must feel, but — "

She spun around. Her eyes were murderous. They froze me in my tracks. "You don't have a clue how I feel, David. But I see through you. And I think what you're trying to do is sick."

"I don't understand — "

"I'm sorry I ever asked you to be on the

staff. You've spent two months staring at me, but I never thought you'd stoop to this. You leave my private life to *me*!"

"But — but — "

I sputtered as she disappeared around the corner. Her footsteps echoed hollowly in the bleak evening.

David Kallas, Master of Tact.

I stood there until my ears became numb with the wind. Then, slowly, I headed home.

My body tensed as I approached the construction site. Smoke was billowing from it now, and I craned my neck to see inside.

The smoke was seeping out of the pipe, escaping upward through the junk in the rotted-open part.

The shoe was gone, of course. But where?

I sat at the edge of the hole. I had seen a foot disappear into a pipe. I had to make sense of it somehow.

I asked myself a basic question: What does a pipe do?

Carry fluids.

How do the fluids move?

From a higher to lower position . . . from higher to lower pressure.

So, an object *in* the pipe — say, a body — would move for the same reasons a liquid would.

Okay, so maybe we had not seen the Foot of the Living Dead. Maybe it had been your garden variety corpse moving to the laws of physics.

Gee, what a relief.

I climbed down into the hole. Using my hands, I cleared out the junk I could see, taking care not to reach into the pipe. Then I lowered my head to look inside.

A billow of smoke rushed around my head, and I came face-to-face with a pair of small eyes.

"Agggh!" I bolted upright.

Footsteps skittered down the pipe, toward the Ramble.

A rat. No big deal. It must have felt worse than I did.

I let my heartbeat settle, then asked myself another small question:

What happens to the contents of a pipe?

They are carried to a dumping place, which in Wetherby is usually the Wampanoag River.

I ran into the Ramble before I had the opportunity to think about what I was doing. Rain had started, and my feet slipped off slick, wet branches.

I found my way to the boulder near the drainpipe. This time, no fuzzy head poked its way out of the water. I leaned out over the river and saw nothing but the gaping black circle of the pipe and some refuse underneath.

As I stood up, the rays of the setting sun caught a shiny object in the muck near the pipe. I walked over, reached in, and pulled out a gold high school ring.

The name RACHEL GREEN was carved on the inside.

Chapter 17

"So how exactly would you date a prehistoric mummy?" asked Mr. O'Toole in first-period physics the next morning. "Mark?"

Rosie looked up from his doodling. "Um . . . ask very nicely?"

The class burst into laughter.

Me? I was barely paying attention. It had been a horrible night. I'd managed to track down Chief Hayes, who had been eating dinner at Arby's with his family. (They were the only customers. The rest of Wetherby had been in hiding every night since Rick had been found.) While they stared at me, chewing away, I had showed him Rachel's ring and explained what had happened.

He had told me not to call the Greens or John Christopher until he'd had a chance to investigate. So I had gone home and faced a ballistic assault from Mom, who was sure I'd been killed. After that I'd called Ariana, who hung up on me. Then I'd had insomnia.

By Friday physics, I was a train wreck. The shock of Rick's death was still in the air, and now Rachel was gone. And John was in my next class, English.

I dreaded going. How could I not tell him? It would be impossible.

I was seriously thinking of giving myself a bloody nose so I could end up in the nurse's office.

Come to think of it, slitting my throat might have been a better idea.

". . . concept of radioactive half-life," Mr. O'Toole droned on. "Who can explain it? David?"

"What?" I muttered.

"Tell me about half-life."

Rachel Green, I wanted to say. That was a half-life. Less. She was only seventeen.

"Okay, I guess Mr. Kallas needs a little jump-start this morning," Mr. O'Toole continued. "David, say I have a radioactive substance that weighs eight ounces. Its half-life is twenty minutes. How heavy will it be in one hour?"

What language was this?

As I sat there, mute and fishlike, Jason Herman was having a cow behind me. "Ooh ooh ooh ooh . . ."

"Jason," Mr. O'Toole said.

"Well, it decays by half each time period. Sixty minutes is three periods, so eight becomes four, then two, then one. The answer is one ounce!"

Mr. O'Toole's face brightened. "Thank you, Jason. Had you answered a few more like that earlier in the semester, you may have pulled ahead of the rest of your classmates."

"Which isn't saying much," said Ed Lyman from the back of the class.

"Hark! He speaks!" Mr. O'Toole said. "The rumors of brain death are not true!"

Somehow I made it to the end of class without further verbal abuse. But as I was walking out, Mr. O'Toole stopped me. "David, I want you to know I will flunk a senior as quickly as a junior. I once hoped you would be my best student. Right now I'll settle for a basic understanding of principles. Got the message?"

"Yes," I said.

This was the latest version of The Speech. The "I Read About Your IQ Score and You're Not Living Up to Your Potential" speech I'd heard many times, in different forms, all four years at school.

Had I known my teachers would expect me to be Einstein, I would have screwed up that test on purpose.

Depressed, I slumped out of class and headed for second period.

I met Jason in the hallway. "You think his wife treats him like that?" Jason asked.

"What?" I walked briskly toward English, and Jason trotted along beside me.

"I read that if a person is mistreated, but feels powerless, he represses his anger, then lets it out at a *safer target* — meaning us! See? It's Freudian."

"Jason, thanks for the analysis, but — "

Jason laughed. "It's not analysis. If it were, I'd be charging you! That'll come in a few years, after I graduate . . . Penn State!"

That was more an announcement than a statement. He was grinning proudly. "Was that the one you were wait-listed at?" I asked.

He nodded. "A local Penn State alum called me at home this morning — and he's meeting me here for lunch, to congratulate me. Amazing, huh? See you!"

He sprinted away, cornering another classmate. I turned left into another hallway.

"David! Wait up!"

My blood ran cold. Goose bumps sprouted on my arms.

Rachel Green was running toward me.

For a dead person, she looked good. Solid. Happy, even.

"Guess what?" she gushed. "Mr. Brophy found out one of his workers wrecked the yearbook! The guy was drunk the night he set the text, and he admitted to it. So Brophy fired . . . what's wrong? Why are you looking at me like that?"

"R-Rachel?" I creaked.

"Y-yes?" It was a cruel imitation.

"I just thought — did Chief Hayes call you last night?"

"Yeah. He brought me this." Rachel held up her left hand to show me her ring. "How did you know?"

"I . . . was the one who found it."

"Well, thanks. That's what I get for exchanging rings with old Pigskinhead." She held up an enormous ring hanging around her neck. "Do I lose *his*? Noooo. Wait till I get my hands on him. You haven't seen him today, have you?"

"No."

"Well, if you do, let him know I'm after him."

"Rachel — " I blurted as she started to run off.

"What?"

My head spun. I tried to picture the foot,

but I couldn't. Was it male? Female? Could it have been John's?

"Earth to David," she said. "Come in."

"Um . . . nothing," I replied.

I ran to English. John was absent. I sat through forty agonizing minutes of William Faulkner, then headed straight for the *Voyager* office.

I punched John's number on the yearbook phone.

"Hello," said a stiff voice. "You have reached the Christopher residence. We cannot come to the phone right now, so — "

I hung up and tried the police station. I was put right through to the chief.

"Hayes."

"This is David Kallas, Chief. I found out that Rachel Green had actually given her ring to a guy named John Christopher. That's C-H-R — "

"David, I know," he interrupted. "We found him."

My throat instantly parched. "Alive?"

"No."

Chapter 18

I dropped the phone.

"David!" Chief Hayes's voice boomed through the room, even from the phone receiver on the floor. *"Are you there?"*

I picked it up. "Uh-huh."

"David, I need your help. Did you know the boy?"

"Uh-huh."

"How about Arnold?"

"A little."

"Can you think of any connection between the two? Were they friends? Enemies? Did they belong to the same teams or clubs?"

"I don't think so."

"Well, call me if you think of anything, okay? I'm working with the parents, but the families don't know each other. Serial killers tend to work in patterns. If we figure it out, we can set a trap."

"Is that what you think this is, a serial killer?"

"Could be. Could also be a copycat who'd read about the killings in 1950."

"What do you *really* think?"

He was silent for a moment, then let out a loud breath. "I wish I could answer that."

"Me, too," I said. "I'll do the best I can, Chief Hayes."

"Thanks. See you, buddy. I know it's hard. Believe me."

I let the phone drop into the cradle. I was numb.

John was my friend. I had known him since second grade.

This was getting too close to home.

I waited for Ariana outside the cafeteria before lunch. That was usually the time we crossed paths.

The cafeteria was at the end of the main hallway. Through the crowd I could see Jason, yammering to a tall, young black guy with a terrible skin condition on his face. I assumed he was the Penn State alumnus. The guy was nodding patiently, probably wondering how the admissions committee could have made such a mistake.

I watched them disappear down a hallway.

Ariana was approaching from the opposite direction.

"I have nothing to say to you," she said as she swept past me into the cafeteria.

I followed behind her. "Ariana, something really horrible has happened — "

"Yeah?" She took a tray and slid it along the metal track. "Well, try not to think about it. A little repression is healthy. You'd be surprised how well it works."

"Ariana — "

"I'm having lunch with *Stephen,* if you don't mind."

"Ariana, John is dead."

Her hand knocked over a salad bowl. She turned to me, her eyes wide with disbelief. "John . . . Christopher?"

"Those feet we saw in the pipe — "

"Oh, no." Her voice was a whisper. Her face blanched.

"We need to talk," I said.

I took her by the arm and left the cafeteria. Just outside the door was a group of seniors, mostly cheerleaders and jocks.

One of them shouted, "The yearbook dudes! Yo, how about this one: Leo Franken, jock and flirt, grinds opponents in the dirt!"

"Hey, you guys keeping the shrunken heads in the new version?" asked another.

I mumbled something and headed the other direction with Ariana. Small groups were hanging out everywhere.

We found a deserted area near a row of lockers. Tears now streamed down Ariana's face.

"Look, I know you're mad at me," I said. "I *was* spying on The Delphic Club, but not just to find out about Smut — uh, *Stephen*. John, Rick, the pipe, that hidden part of the basement — they're all connected somehow. We have to get involved in this, for John's sake, at least. Now, Chief Hayes thinks there might be — "

The clatter of footsteps made me stop. Three girls were heading toward us, deep in conversation.

Behind me was the backstage door to the auditorium. I pulled it open, and we walked onto the empty stage. " — a serial killer," I went on as the door slammed shut behind us.

"Oh, great," Ariana replied. "So who's next?"

"Well, *if* you believe that's true, we need to think of a pattern of murder."

"What do you mean, *if*? What else could it be?"

"I — I don't know. I think something much weirder than that is going on here — "

132

"Oh. Like what? Something *paranormal*, David?"

I shrugged. "Well . . ."

"A ghost?" Ariana was looking at me sharply. "Or maybe a dead dog come back to life? You've been reading too much Stephen King, David. If some murderer is on the loose here — "

"Yeeeeaagh!"

The scream cut Ariana off. It was muffled, and directly below us.

"Oh, my god," I said.

"Come on!" Ariana ran to the spiral stairs and threw open the gate. We practically tripped over each other to get to the basement.

The scenery shop light was on. The bookcase had been swung open.

We barged into the cavern. The scream rang out again, much louder. This time I recognized the voice.

"Jason!" I called out.

The graffiti swirled past us. We rounded corner after corner, following the voice. The basement seemed endless, opening again and again, into areas not visible from the bookcase. My blood pounded now. A mist swirled around us, and the chalky smell invaded my nostrils.

"Where are we going?" Ariana yelled.

"I don't know!" I was ahead of Ariana now, and turning to answer her, I only saw mist.

"*Help! Don't let him do this to me!*"

We were close — just *how* close was impossible to tell.

"Where are you, Jason!" I bellowed.

"*AAAAAAAGGHHHHHHH!*"

To my left. About twenty feet. I pushed through the soupy mist. I couldn't see the floor, and I felt as if I were floating.

"David!"

Ariana's call seemed to come from under a blanket.

"Here!" I answered.

I was shocked by the immediate touch of her hand on my arm. She was right behind me.

A long, wide, darkness appeared, almost invisible. As I came closer, it solidified, took the form of a gash in the ground.

My knees locked. I had gotten too close, standing inches from the edge. The crack was enormous now, at least six feet wide. It spewed huge, cumulus puffs of smoke in irregular rhythms.

And between each one was a view of the bottom. A churning mass of yellowish-white, not purely liquid or solid or gas, but somehow all of them interchanging.

I became aware of Ariana's hand in mine. I did not need to look at her face. I felt the shock through her fingers.

"No-o-o-o-o-o-o!"

Jason's voice was to my right.

I took only five steps. Smoke exploded in my face and dissipated like dancing fingers. When it cleared, I saw Jason.

Tendrils twined around him, pocked and lumpy like stone, yet somehow elastic and fluid. They pulsed rhythmically, glistening with a whitish ooze. His arms were pinned to his sides, his legs half sunken into the crevice.

"David, let's get out of here," Ariana pleaded.

Every human instinct told me Ariana was right. My brain was shooting flight commands to my legs. But I could not move. A part of me felt drawn to the hole. My body felt an energy pure and powerful, my mind a jolt of awakening.

Jason's face now registered nothing. But as he slowly twisted, sinking into the hole, his eyes caught sight of us and flickered with recognition.

Under the tendrils, his hand fumbled frantically. He managed to reach into his pocket and throw its contents to the ground. Scraps of paper floated on a current of smoke and landed near the edge of the crevice.

A garbled sound escaped his mouth. The word was unintelligible, but the intent was clear.

Jason's plea for help would be his last if Ariana and I just stood there.

I stepped toward him, breaking the hold of logic and fear.

"David, are you crazy?" Ariana cried.

I did not answer. My knees bent, and I sprang toward Jason, who was now under the floor surface.

Arms wide, I hurtled into the abyss.

Chapter 19

Stiletto pain.

Harsh, ripping, stretching. Pulling my body in all directions, like dough.

My vision blurred. I felt my fingertips a mile below my toes, my knees behind my head. I blinked and felt a shot of electricity carom through my brain, which now felt as if it were the size of a football field.

I was neither standing nor falling. I saw only white-yellow, the color of the tendrils and bubbling mass at the bottom of the crevice.

Words echoed and overlapped, building into shrieks, sobs, and babbles. Some were mine, some Ariana's and Jason's.

But most of the voices were completely unfamiliar, shifting in and out of English with the fury of a cyclone. I tried to cover my ears, but I couldn't tell where my hands were.

Then, without warning, the voices stopped.

I felt my body snap together like a rubber band. I still saw nothing, and I lurched about like a leaf on the wind.

But my fear was disappearing now. I felt peace covering me, massaging me. I began to soar, forgetting about anyone but myself. Soon all my thoughts seemed to be swallowed up, and I was in a state of blissful emptiness.

You're early.

I didn't exactly *hear* the words. They seemed to plant themselves inside me, in some mental place I'd never been before. I tried to move my mouth, but I couldn't feel it. Instead I thought the question *Where am I?*

A small giggle was the response. Then, *The omphalos, daddy-o. Try that on for size.*

The voice — if you could call it that — was male. Young, too, as if it belonged to someone my age.

Where's my friend? I thought.

Silence. Mumbling. And then another, older, male voice: *He was needed.*

And me? I asked. *I'm needed, too?*

In a different way, David, answered someone distinctly female. *First, go back. Your task is to find out who we are. If you do, you will earn your place.*

What if I don't?

I felt a low, agitated rumble.

We've delivered all we can of the message, the female answered. *Now, go.*

Wait a minute —

The first voice cut me off: *Do it. Dig?*

And then a hand grabbed my arm, and the floating stopped. So did the voices. I heard screaming, muffled at first, and then piercing. I was yanked upward, and found myself sprawled on a dirt floor.

When I looked up, the mist had become thin. I could make out the basement walls.

"David?"

Ariana was gaping at me, her face streaked with black, sooty tears.

"Whoa . . . " I said. "What just happened?"

"I don't know," she replied. "But it turned your hair white."

Chapter 20

Screech!

A driver's ed car swerved to avoid Ariana and me as we bolted out the back door and into the school parking lot. The teacher bellowed profanities, but we barely heard them.

We didn't stop running until we reached the police station.

As we described our experience to Chief Hayes, he listened blankly, as if we were speaking Swedish.

"Let me get this straight," he said, scratching his head and leaning forward on his swivel chair. "You did not actually see any of these people. You just heard them."

"Right," I replied.

"And, you, Ariana, you didn't hear a thing?"

"No, but I saw what happened to Jason!"

"The smoke and the snakes."

"They were more like tentacles," Ariana said.

"Tentacles. Uh-huh." Chief Hayes was smoking again. He exhaled and played with a pencil. He looked as if he were trying to remember where he kept the straitjackets. "Now, David, did these . . . *voices* sound familiar to you?"

"Nope. Two of them sounded really old-fashioned, almost British. The other one was definitely American. He was trying to sound cool, but he got it all wrong. He actually said stuff like, 'You dig?' and 'Daddy-o.' "

"Ancient," Chief Hayes grumbled. "People talked like that when *I* was in high school."

"Exactly."

Chief Hayes raised an eyebrow and spread out the papers Ariana had collected — the ones Jason had thrown to the ground. "And these mean nothing to you."

Ariana and I looked at it all again: receipts from a cash machine and Write Bros. stationery store; a gum wrapper; and a business card belonging to someone named George Derbin from AccuByte, a nearby software company.

"Well, Jason was talking with some guy in a jacket and tie in the lobby just before this all happened," I said. "Maybe that was George Derbin."

Chief Hayes took the card and pressed the speaker button on his phone. The dial tone droned, and he punched the number on the card.

"Hello, you have reached the AccuByte electronic voice-message service," a recorded voice blared over the speaker. "If you would like to leave a message for a specific person, please enter the first three letters of that person's name. Otherwise — "

Beep. Beep. Beep.

"Thank you. There is no one at AccuByte with the letters of the name requested. If you would like to try a different — "

Chief Hayes slammed the receiver down and typed in some letters on his computer. While the hard drive burbled, he riffled through the pages of a phone book.

"Hmm, nothing in the white pages or the police files under Derbin," he mumbled. "David, what did this guy in the hallway look like?"

"Young, black, not much older than us, really tall and skinny. His face was a little . . . I don't know, distorted, I guess. Lumpy. Bad skin. Jason had told me he was supposed to meet some Penn State alumnus, so I figured that was him."

"And he was not in the basement when you got there?" he asked.

"Even if he was, we wouldn't have seen him," Ariana said. "The fog was too thick."

"He might have been sucked down into the hole, too," I suggested.

"That still doesn't explain what either of them was doing down there in the first place," the chief said. "Is that part of the basement *used* for anything these days?"

"This group called The Delphic Club meets there," I answered. "I mean, it's supposed to be a secret — "

Chief Hayes's eyes bore into mine. "What do they do?"

"I'm not sure. Supposedly talk about philosophy and poetry — "

"Do they sing?"

Ariana and I exchanged a blank look. "I don't think so," I said. "Why?"

Chief Hayes shrugged. "The acoustics are great down there," he muttered.

"Look, I know you don't believe us," Ariana said, "but if you're looking for some easy explanation — "

"I'm not." Chief Hayes slumped back with a weary sigh. He put his fingers to his brow and stayed that way for a long time. Just when

I thought he had passed into a nap, he looked up. "I went down into that basement in my senior year, after the search for my friend was called off, and before they sealed the trick wall. I was so angry — I thought for sure I'd find clues of KKK meetings or something. I figured all those people who suspected Communist or Fascist groups were just wrong. . . . Well, they were. But so was I."

"What did you find?" Ariana asked.

"A singing group," he said. "All seniors, all dressed up in togas and stuff, very weird. They seemed happy to see me and pulled me over to teach me the song. I didn't want to, but they all grabbed me. I panicked and fought back. Next thing I knew, I was alone, flat on my back in the dark. I got up and tried to run out, but my ankle was hurt. Eventually it developed a bone spur and never healed."

"Which is why you limp," I said.

"That's right." Chief Hayes lifted his left pantleg and rolled down his sock to reveal a golfball-size growth. "Let me ask you, David. Did you have that bump on your forehead before you went into the basement?"

My fingers flew upward. I groped around and discovered a small hard lump on my right temple. "Whoa . . . this is new. I guess I must have hit my head."

Chief Hayes reached out and touched my forehead. "It's rock-hard. Bone. This is no ordinary bump. I believe you have a calcium growth, just like my ankle spur."

"You think there's some connection?" Ariana asked.

"I'm thinking aloud." Chief Hayes began pacing. "The face of this Derbin guy . . . you described it as lumpy."

I nodded. "Yeah, like he had some sort of disease."

"Did you ever see the movie *The Elephant Man*?"

"About the guy with the deformed body," Ariana said.

"He was a victim of neurofibromatosis," Chief Hayes went on. "A buildup of calcium all over his body."

"So you think there's a connection between what *Derbin* has and what we have," I said.

"And maybe Derbin is connected to whatever is in the basement," Ariana continued. "He may have *led* Jason there!"

"We need to figure out who this guy is," Chief Hayes said.

"How?" I asked.

"I can run a check throughout the nearby precincts. If I don't find anything, I can try to get access to FBI information. In the meantime, we try to work on the name itself. My hunch is it's an alias. If so, the name itself may contain a clue. People pick aliases for a reason — sometimes consciously, sometimes not. A person from Texas might call himself Dallas, for example. Another might scramble the letters of his name, or borrow his mom's maiden name, or name himself after something in his neighborhood, like a restaurant or street. Is there a Derbin Avenue in some nearby town, or a Derbin diner?"

"We can work on that," I said. Ariana nodded in agreement.

Chief Hayes stood near his desk. "Fine. And promise me two things: You won't talk about this to *anybody*, and you won't do a thing related to this case without consulting me."

"It's a deal," I said.

"Deal," Ariana agreed.

"Let me warn you. Things are going to get rough around here this weekend. I issued a public statement about John Christopher's death an hour ago. Expect panic, and lots of crazy talk." Chief Hayes took a deep breath. "And I'm sorry . . . about your friend."

Ariana looked at the floor.

"So are we," I managed to say.

*　　*　　*

When I walked into my house, I saw myself in the living room mirror. Ariana had exaggerated. My hair was not *all* white.

Actually, it was still mostly brown. I guess you'd call it salt-and-pepper.

I couldn't help grinning. It looked kind of cool.

My mom was asleep on the couch. On her chest was a photo album.

I gently lifted it. It was open to old photos of her and my dad on their honeymoon in Greece. I couldn't help leafing through.

They looked young and happy, grinning in front of restaurants, beaches, and tons of different ruins. Each photo had a brief caption, carefully written in my mother's handwriting: SOAKING UP HISTORY AT THE PARTHENON; FOLLOWING IN THE FOOTSTEPS OF PERICLES; THE LABYRINTH AT KNOSSOS; THE ORACLE AT THE TEMPLE OF APOLLO, DELPHI.

My eyes locked on that last picture. Mom and Dad had their arms around each other. Behind them were half-buildings and cracked walls.

Under it was written THE OMPHALOS.

"David?"

My mom's eyes flickered open. She looked at me, blinking.

"Hi, Mom." I held up the album, pointing to the picture. "What's this?"

"David, what on Earth did you do to your hair — and your forehead?"

I had figured this out on the way home. "We were playing around with hair dye. We're doing a skit — the staff, I mean. I'm going to play Mr. DeWaart. And, uh, I bumped my head in gym. Klutz, huh? So. What does *omphalos* mean?"

Raising a suspicious eyebrow, she took the book from my hand and looked at it. "Belly button."

"What?"

She smiled. "The Ancient Greeks thought Delphi was the center of the world. A famous oracle lived there, and it was protected by Apollo, the god of music and poetry. People came from all over to have their fortunes told. Songs were sung day and night — Apollo's spirit rubbed off, I guess. Anyway, Delphi became known as the *omphalos*, which was another way of saying 'the center.' "

"You think this was all true?" I asked.

Mom laughed. "The problem was, a special priestess had to translate the oracle's messages, because the oracle was really a vein of gas that hissed up through the ground. It probably sounded to the Greeks like whispers."

"Gas, huh?" I said. "A legend out of mystical Earth farts."

"Something like that." She got up from the couch and yawned. "Now come help me with dinner. And please wash that stuff out of your hair."

"I . . . kind of like it," I replied, promising myself I'd get some brown hair dye.

That night I could not get to sleep. The voice had told me I was at the omphalos. What did that mean? I mean, *Wetherby,* the center of the world? Please. Maybe they truly meant the belly button. The Lint Catcher of the World. That was more like it.

I flicked on the night-light and grabbed a used envelope out of my trash can. On top I wrote:

GEORGE DERBIN

I began playing around with the letters. I came up with:

GREG DREIBONE
ROGER BEIGEND
BEN RIDGE GOER
NERO GEBRIDGE
ED EGO BRINGER

ONE BIRD EGGER
GREED OR BINGE
GREEN DOG BRIE
BEER IN DE GROG

It was getting ridiculous, and my eyes were shutting — until I wrote:

REGGIO BENDER

I sat up. I quickly rearranged a few letters and came up with another name. The name of a person I knew about but had never met, a person who matched the description of George Derbin, minus the growths on his face.

One by one, I checked the letters to make sure I hadn't slipped one in or dropped one.

When I was sure I hadn't, I stared at the name until it burned itself in my eyes.

REGGIE BORDEN

I almost didn't get to sleep that night. But I did.

And I dreamed.

PART SIX

Mark

Chapter 21

"Hold his arm, Garvin," the police lieutenant says to the young police officer, who is so pretty Mark has the urge to ask her out.

And he might have, if they hadn't at that moment been in the city morgue.

He braces himself. Another officer slowly pulls open a drawer. No one has said exactly who he is supposed to identify. And even though Mark has only one family member — unless you count his mom and dad, who he still thinks are alive somewhere — he holds out hope the drawer will hold a stranger. He will shake his head no, walk out, and suggest dinner and a very sexy movie to Officer Garvin. He wonders how old she is. Probably early twenties.

The cadaver is short. The other officer efficiently pulls back the white sheet, sending a puff of icy smoke in the air.

Mark feels suddenly congested, as if he can't breathe.

Officer Garvin squeezes his arm. Mark feels his knees buckle.

"It's my grandmother," he manages to say. He turns to the lieutenant, who looks either bored or solemn. "How did it happen?" Mark asks.

"A bus," the lieutenant says. "It was very sudden. No one exactly saw her get in front of it."

Mark understands what that meant. She was old. She couldn't judge distances. Her reflexes were bad.

It was her fault.

Officer Garvin helps him into another room, which is empty except for a few metal chairs, a table, and a wall phone. She is holding some stapled-together pieces of paper, which she drops onto the table.

Mark sits. He watches the room circle around him and blur.

The tears surprise him. He hasn't cried in years. Twelve, to be exact — since before his parents' funeral service. He had clammed up that day — no crying, no words, nothing. His Yiayia had been frightened by his behavior. But nobody had understood the truth, that his mom and dad were still alive. Somewhere. So what was the use of looking sad? It would only make everyone else believe the lie even more.

But he has just seen Yiayia. She is dead. And the sight of her makes him think — for the first time — that maybe his parents are, too.

It gushes out. Years of buried anger and hurt and fear and love and sorrow. He weeps, heaving his shoulders. He is alone now.

"What — what's going to happen to me?" he asks between sobs.

"We'll have to notify your next of kin — an aunt, uncle, another grandparent — "

Mark shakes his head. "My grandfathers are both dead. My other grandmother lives on a Greek island and doesn't speak English, my mom's sister is in a religious cult, and my dad was an only child."

"I see." Officer Garvin sits back in her chair. "Mark, how old are you?"

"Seventeen."

She drums her fingers on the table, then picks up the phone. "Garvin here. Can I have Social Services?"

When she gets off the phone, Mark asks, "Do I have to be sent to an orphanage or something?"

"No. But until you're eighteen, you need a guardian. We'll help find you a good foster family — people who have experience with teens."

Mark isn't hearing her words. He stares at

the top sheet of the papers she has put on the desk. It is loaded with blank lines. Only one of them is filled in.

He tries to focus. He blinks, and the handwriting becomes clear. After DATE OF DEATH someone has scribbled today's date: January 11, 2016.

A tear lands on the "J." Mark watches it soak in and spread the ink in a star shape. Officer Garvin is still talking. He can tell she is crying, too.

Later. A couple of weeks, maybe. Mark is staying at the house of a friend, Jon Feldman. He stumbles out of bed when Mrs. Feldman calls him to the phone.

"Yeah?" he grunts into the receiver.

"Hi, Mark? It's Officer Garvin."

And I'm going to adopt you and we can play house together, Mark wants her to say.

No such luck. "We've found a family," she goes on. "Or a father, at least. His name is Walter Ojeda. He's a widower, he's really nice, and he lives close enough so you can finish out senior year in your school if you want."

"What's close enough?"

"Two towns over. Wetherby."

"I don't want to live in that hole."

"You'd be surprised. They've rebuilt that town

from the ground up, ever since the chemical company opened."

"I know. My parents worked there."

"Great! Look, I know you'll do terrifically. Anyway, Mr. Ojeda will be coming to visit you at the Feldmans' tonight. Would you like me to fax you a holo of him?"

"I guess."

"Okay. Bye. And don't worry."

"Right. Bye."

Mark waits by the fax until it spits out a color hologram of Walter Ojeda. He looks older than Mark expects him to. He's kind of stern-looking, but it's hard to tell for sure behind the beard.

Plus he has this growth on his cheek. Mark doesn't know why, but that bothers him.

PART SEVEN

David

Chapter 22

I woke up in a cold sweat. My dream was breaking up into fragments of memory, and I didn't try to hold on to them.

My clock said 9:07. I'd gone to sleep at sunrise, 6:00 or so.

Three fat hours. I was going to be in great shape today.

It didn't matter. I had work to do. Lots of it.

I was dressed in seconds. Quietly I opened my door and heard my mom's snores from her room. I tiptoed downstairs and punched Ariana's number on the kitchen phone.

She picked up in the middle of the first ring. She was sobbing. "I'm sorry! Oh, I'm so glad you called. I . . . I love you so much. Please come over. Please!"

"Sure, Ariana," I replied softly. "I'll be right there."

"*David?*"

"Uh-huh."

She groaned. "I thought you were Stephen! Ohhhh, I feel like such an *idiot*! Why did you do that to me?"

"Uh, Ariana, you didn't even wait to hear my voice."

"Okay, okay. What do you want?"

"I need to talk to you. I know who George Derbin is."

"Really? Who?"

"Reggie Borden."

The phone fell silent. "Ariana," I continued, "are you still there?"

"Yeah. I must be half-asleep, though, because I thought I heard you say George Derbin was Reggie Borden. Silly me."

"That *is* what I said. The names are anagrams of each other. Derbin was young, thin, black, and incredibly tall — just like Reggie. The photos of Reggie look a lot like the guy I saw with Jason — except George Derbin had those growths on his face."

"Oh, this is too weird. I'm not hearing this."

"Ariana, remember in Chief Hayes's office, when you suggested that Jason had been led into the basement?"

"Yeah, I suggested *George Derbin* had led him. What are you saying? That Reggie Borden actually hibernated underground all these years, like Rip Van Winkle?"

"If he did, he'd be Chief Hayes's age."

"Oh! He's been in suspended animation! Okay, that explains it. Whew, for a minute I was confused."

I ignored Ariana's sarcasm. "Just listen to me. One of the voices used fifties slang, and he sounded our age. I know it seems far-fetched, but — "

"You think one of the *voices* was Reggie's? He brought Jason down and then hopped back in the hole with two ghost buddies?"

"Jason was desperate to get us George Derbin's business card. He must have been trying to warn us."

Ariana didn't answer.

"You can't deny what you *saw*, Ariana! Is my theory any less believable than a crack in the earth that spits out smoke and slime monsters?"

"No, I guess not. Go on."

"Okay. The voices said they were delivering a message. From whom?"

"The slime monster," Ariana said dryly.

"Must be. And this *thing* takes people, roto-roots them from the inside — "

"*Gross*, David."

"Sorry. It wasted no time gobbling up Rick,

John, and Jason — but it spares others. It hasn't touched the Delphic Club members, who hold their meetings practically on top of it. It didn't do anything to Chief Hayes in 1950, or to you and me. I *dove* into its hole — and even then it didn't want me. It gave me back."

"Because you were *too early* — that's what you said *it* said," Ariana reminded me. "Maybe it's going through the whole school in some strange order."

"The voices want me to find out who they are," I barged on. "They're testing me."

"Why?"

"I'm not sure, but I have an idea." I took a deep breath. "In 1950, the same time Reggie disappeared, three other kids showed up dead. Reggie was never found . . . until now."

"The thing *kept* him," Ariana said.

"And I think it wants to keep me — make me into a fourth . . . voice."

"Oh, great. So this is some kind of aptitude test for admission to zombieland? They think you're stupid enough to want to join them — "

"I am."

"What? Stupid?"

"No! Don't you see? I have to do it. If I find out about them, I might find out about the monster. This whole thing might come together — the earthquake, the murders, everything."

"I was wrong. You're not stupid. You're insane."

"What's the alternative? Staying ignorant and letting more people die?"

"You saw your forehead, David. You're developing a growth, like Chief Hayes. How long before you look like this . . . *ghost* of Reggie Borden? What if you *and* Chief Hayes are turning into zombies?"

"I'm not turning into anything, Ariana. Chief Hayes doesn't remember exactly what happened to him in the basement. But he escaped, just as I did. He went on to live a long, normal life — and so will I. We were — *infected* in some way, but obviously not enough."

"How do you know that? This could transform you slowly, over years. *How do we even know Chief Hayes is on our side?*"

"Ariana, we can't get paranoid about this."

"I can get as paranoid as I want!"

I couldn't tell whether or not Ariana was crying.

"We can't bring John and Jason and Rick back," I said softly. "But we owe them a little effort. If we can figure out *why* they were chosen, we may be able to predict who's next."

Ariana sighed. "Okay. You're right. I — I shouldn't be giving you a hard time."

"So you'll help me?" I asked.

"Yeah, I'll come over in a few minutes."

"No. Meet me at the library. I want to look at the town history again. The thing was here in 1950, and it took Reggie. But no one else disappeared that year — "

"So you think the other two voices were taken at another time, and you want to check for earthquakes and strange disappearances and murders."

"You got it."

"Hey, I didn't get to be editor in chief for nothing." Ariana gave a weak laugh. "But here's what I want to know: Say this thing wakes up every few years, just belches out of the ground, makes everybody's life miserable, eats people like flies. Then why does it go back to sleep? Does it get too full? Does it have some fatal weakness?"

"Maybe it's allergic to females."

"Ha-ha. Keep it up. I guess you enjoy going to the library alone."

"Meet you there in ten minutes?"

"Let me call Stephen back. We had this fight before you called. We were supposed to hang out this afternoon, but he called to say he couldn't make it."

"How come?"

"Well . . . that's what I need to find out. I figured it had something to do with Monique, so I hung up on him."

My heart started pumping. *Now* she would get angry at him. "Okay, work it out. I'll see you in twenty minutes?"

"Make it a half-hour."

"Twenty-five."

"David — "

"Bye."

Chapter 23

"David, you look awful."

Mrs. Klatsch greeted me with those words as I barged into the library. I did not bother to return the compliment.

Needless to say, on a Saturday morning, the place was not crowded. At the nearest table, I dropped my backpack, which contained a copy of the *Voyager*, my alphabetical list of the Wetherby High School senior class, my notebook full of clippings, and a pen.

"Oh . . . yeah, a skit. It's dye," I replied. "Bumped my head, too — "

"David, I'm sorry about your classmates. It must be awful — "

"Mm-hm." I tried not to let my impatience show. "Um, may I use the Wetherby history book?"

She looked at me as if I were insane. "Sure, David," she mumbled, pulling the book out of the stacks behind her desk. "More earthquake research?"

"Sort of," I replied.

"Well, if I can be of any help . . ."

"Thanks." I tried to give as normal-looking a smile as possible. She didn't seem convinced.

I took the book and placed it next to my other stuff. I'd forgotten to bring a pad of paper, so I turned over my student list and stared at the blank page.

Now what?

I hate blank pages. They make me dizzy. That's because I stare at them a lot, especially when I have to do papers. I get tired. I get nauseated. I stand up, walk around, and end up at a large electric object, like a refrigerator or TV.

I couldn't do that now. I picked up my pencil and wrote:

VOICE 1 = BORDEN

Genius. Brilliant. A+. Skip a grade.

What did I think I was doing? I knew nothing.

I looked at my watch, then the door. I hoped Ariana was off the phone by now.

I took a deep breath that ended as a yawn. Mrs. Klatsch glared at me.

Okay, Kallas. Chill. Start at the beginning.

Victims:

*ARNOLD CHRISTOPHER
HERMAN ... NEXT ?
SABOTAGED YEARBOOK POEMS:
  LYMAN YOUMANS HEALD
  CHASE ... WHY ?
YEARS:
  1994 1950 ... ANY OTHERS ?*

Duh.

Sherlock Holmes was laughing in his grave. Splitting his sides. Choking on his pipe.

I opened *Our Town: A Wetherby History from 1634 to the Present* to the end. Then I slowly made my way backward through the years, looking for anything suspicious.

Hot stuff. In 1977, the mayor's bathroom caught fire. A kid was jailed for wearing long hair to school in 1969. A meteor fell on a car in 1958. The Blizzard of '44 swallowed a house. Teddy Roosevelt visited in '03. Zzzzzzz.

When I was into the nineteenth century, I stopped at a drawing. In it, a group of people, blacks and whites, stood by a large hole in the ground. A woman was on a podium, reading from a sheet of paper.

Under the drawing, it said:

Poet Clara Farnham delivering her eulogy to a local hero, April 8, 1862:

A nation riven, rent by strife,
Can deem none of its men more free
Than he who gives a life for life
In service of Equality.
Who scoffs at Fortune, risks disaster,
Pulls from tunnel dark and drear,
His fellow man, once slave to master?
'Tis such a one we honor here.
Let us then, 'ere we depart,
Now consecrate this hallowed site
To him of stout and noble heart,
Beloved neighbor, Jonas Lyte.

I read further. It was the usual stuff, Lyte the abolitionist, Lyte the rescuer of slaves. Then I came to this passage:

> Scandal, sabotage, and weather hampered Lyte's efforts. Several slaves were found dead in the tunnel he had built, along with some of Lyte's workers. Lyte himself died inside the tunnel when part of it collapsed during a storm. Workers dug

for days, but Lyte's body was
not found.

Bingo.
My heart started to pound.
I knew where Lyte had gone. He had built
his tunnel in the wrong place. He wanted to
help the slaves, but he met ol' Slimy instead.
And Slimy kept him.

VOICE 2 = JONAS LYTE

Yes. It had to be.
I added the new date to the others:

1994   1950   1862

I began flipping through the book again.
Smallpox epidemic, riots, the Revolutionary
War, witch-hunts. Deaths galore.
My eyes were crossing. What did this
mean? Slimy could have been around the whole
time. Maybe it caused the war. Maybe it
spread the smallpox. (Was *that* what I had?)
I slumped back in my seat. A gust of wind
came through a window and flipped a page. I
slapped my hand down to stop it.
My right index finger had landed on the nose
of Annabelle Spicer. Fortunately she didn't
seem to mind.

I took my hand away and looked at the picture that Ariana had banned from the yearbook. It was labeled 1686. Annabelle's wide eyes stared past me, defiant and innocent. As she burned at the stake, watched by the cackling devil, plumes of smoke rose from what looked like a black cloak on the ground. Her executioners looked on in horror. Some townspeople were falling to their knees. Others, mostly young, were dancing and singing.

I needed some comic relief. I smiled. I read about the witch-hunts, the quotes about "crag-faced hags" and "demented children" and "secret lairs."

And as I turned the page, my eye caught the smoking black cloak again. I wondered what was in it. Dry ice? Burning rubber?

I glanced toward the clock. Mrs. Klatsch was climbing down a spiral staircase into the library's storage area below. I had a sudden urge to pull her back. Spiral staircases into basements were making me nervous.

That was when I knew.

I looked at the picture again. My mouth dropped open.

It wasn't a black cloak.

It was a gash. In the ground.

The third voice was female.

I scribbled Annabelle Spicer's name.

"Yes!" I cried out.

On a chair to my left, an old man awoke with a start and dropped his newspaper.

I wrote:

$$1994 \quad 1950 \quad 1862 \quad 1686$$

Was there a pattern?

I was suddenly gripped with acute stomach pain. Waves of nausea.

I was going to have to use math.

And I did. Without a calculator. Sweaty palms and all.

The first two dates were 44 years apart. The next two were 88, and the next 176.

The gaps were shrinking by half.

Half-life.

"And the thigh bone's connected to the hip bone," I sang to myself as I figured out the remaining gaps. I filled in my time line all the way back to 778 B.C. I felt like continuing back to the Jurassic Era, but I cut it short. Wetherby was settled in 1634, so anything earlier was useless.

The library clock said 11:43. Ariana was late.

But it didn't matter. I was on a roll.

On a hunch, I turned over the student list and circled the names of the three victims.

Hmmm . . .

I counted the letters in the three victims' names: 13, 15, 11.

Dead end.

I said the names aloud. I tried rearranging letters.

Then I ripped out each entry, including all three columns: alphabetical number, the name, and method of payment:

11   ARNOLD, RICHARD   —
22   CHRISTOPHER, JOHN   CASH
44   HERMAN, JASON   CK

"Oh my lord . . ."

Slimy kept its patterns simple.

First dates, than student numbers.

All ending in death.

I tried to swallow, but my throat felt as if I'd stuffed a sock into it. As I lifted a page of the list, my hands shook.

The next victim was Lucky Number 88.

Words and numbers floated on the page. I blinked and tried to focus.

Then I saw the name.

88   MAAS, ARIANA   CK

Chapter 24

My eyes shot toward the clock.

12:15.

Ariana should have been at the library by now.

Where was she? I had to warn her.

I fumbled around in my pocket for change for the pay phone. I was broke.

I caught a glimpse of Mrs. Klatsch walking up the spiral staircase.

"Mrs. Klatsch," I said, barely containing my voice. "Can I use your phone for a local call?"

"*Qui . . . et . . . ly.*"

I grabbed the receiver and punched Ariana's number.

No answer.

Easy, David, I told myself. Keep it together. Think.

She'd said she was going to call Smut, to

straighten out their argument. Something unexpected must have happened.

Under Mrs. Klatsch's disapproving gaze, I tapped Smut's number on the phone.

" 'lo?"

"Hi, Lily?" (Lily is Smut's eleven-year-old sister.)

"Yeah."

"Can I speak to your brother?"

"He left."

"Do you know where he went?"

"Uh-uh."

"Was anyone with him?" I asked.

"Uh . . . yeah."

I wanted to strangle her. "Who?"

"That guy. The yearbook teacher. He picked Stephen up."

"*Mr. DeWaart?*"

"I guess."

"Lily, was Ariana with them?"

"Uh-uh. She called too late."

"You mean, she called your house after they left?"

"Yeah."

"And you told her where Smut had gone?"

"Huh? Who's *Smut*?"

"No one. Thanks."

I slammed the receiver down. I stuffed my

books and papers into my backpack, slung it over my shoulder, and bolted toward the front door.

"Is something wrong?" Mrs. Klatsch called out.

"I'll tell you later!" I shouted.

I raced out of the library. I knew where Ariana had gone. After she talked to Lily, she panicked. She assumed The Delphic Club was having a meeting — and she went to head them off at the high school.

To warn Smut. To protect him.

Instead, she was walking right into a death-trap.

My feet pounded the pavement. I could feel the blood rising to my face, gorging behind my eyes. I was furious at Smut, furious at Ariana, and scared out of my mind at what might be happening.

Screeeak!

I was in the street. I saw headlights. I heard a horn. A scream.

Then I felt myself flying. Briefly.

I landed on the sidewalk. Behind me I heard the sound of shattering glass.

"Are you all right?"

A balding man in a tweed jacket was looking at me with a pale expression. Two cars had jumped the curb and hit a light post. One driver was cursing a blue streak.

"Yeah. Fine."

I was halfway down the block when I heard police sirens.

The school parking lot was a straight three-block run. Mr. DeWaart's car was sitting there. Just beyond it, one of the school's back doors was propped open with a trash can. I ran inside and snaked through the hallways to the backstage door. Yanking it open, I headed for the spiral staircase.

I could hear singing as I started to descend. I had never heard the tune. It was beautiful, but it sent a chill up my spine.

I clattered to the bottom and raced through the open bookcase. I rounded the corners, sped through the grafitti-covered chambers. The mist was swirling, spiraling at my side, seeming to point me in the right direction.

Then, suddenly, I saw them.

The Delphic Club. Singing at the top of their lungs, each member dressed identically in gray, flowing robes. Their arms were linked, and they swayed back and forth to the tune.

I stopped in my tracks. I was in their line of vision, but no one seemed to notice me.

Their eyes were glazed. They seemed to be under some spell. *What were they doing?*

Just beyond them, clouds of smoke spewed upward from the crevice. From their midst emerged a black form, smiling, arms held upward.

I recognized Mr. DeWaart's face before he saw me. In the dim light, his beard seemed thickly sinister, his face cragged and shadowy. He sang with the swaying group, in a deep baritone.

"Wartface," I said under my breath.

Mr. DeWaart stopped singing. His eyes betrayed no surprise as he looked at me. "I have always found that nickname puerile."

"But they're not warts, are they?"

He smiled. "Not any more than the one on your forehead."

Suddenly more pieces of the puzzle had fallen into place. I stared at Mr. DeWaart, trying to put my mounting anger into words. "You *were* the one — "

A scream cut me off. Even in the soupy murk, it was earsplitting.

And it was unmistakably Ariana's.

"*No!*" I bellowed.

"Stay here, David," Mr. DeWaart said with eerie calmness. "You can't change destiny."

I ran past him. The smoke enveloped me,

smothered me with its chalky sweetness. I pushed through, fighting for breath.

Ariana was shrieking my name.

I followed her voice, groping at the cloud with my arms. "I'm here!"

I saw the crevice, a vague dark line in the whiteness. Ariana was nearby. I flailed blindly in the direction of her voice.

Then I touched something.

Cold. Wet. Clammy smooth. And pulsing.

I tried to yank my hand back, but the snake was wrapping itself around my wrist.

I grabbed it with my other hand and pulled. My fingers slipped off, coated with a drippy white ooze.

On the smoke-slickened floor, my feet began sliding toward the hole. I dropped to my knees.

"David! *David!*" Ariana screamed. "I see you!"

I opened my mouth, but no sound came out. Something was around my chest now. Squeezing, lifting me off the ground.

I floated over the crevice. In the eddies of smoke I could see a flickering form. It grew closer, jerking frantically.

"*A — ri — ana!*" I rasped.

She was clear now, between the cottony puffs. The tentacles had trapped her like a vine around a fence post. Through the maze I could see her eyes, sparked with anger.

Her teeth flashed briefly. With a savage thrust, she buried them in the fleshy skin of the tendril.

White-yellow goop exploded in a fountain. The tendril recoiled from Ariana, ripping itself from her mouth.

What followed was beyond noise. The blast of agonized sound boxed my ears. The tentacle that had wrapped me suddenly loosened. My torso slipped downward, out of its clutches.

I was falling freely, through a sea of writhing tendrils, with nothing below to catch me.

I blacked out, and my blind panic began to splinter and fall away, replaced by a gathering dream.

PART EIGHT

Mark

Chapter 25

Benign tumors.

Irregular growth.

Crowding cranial nerves.

Inoperable.

"Maybe you shouldn't be reading that stuff."

Mark hasn't heard his foster father enter the room. Walter Ojeda looks concerned. He surveys the open boxes of papers and books — all stuff Mark had found in the attic of his parents' house.

For years the attic door had been padlocked, but the movers had been only too happy to help Mark break the lock. They had not been quite so happy to move the cardboard boxes Mark had found upstairs, which were black with mildew, gnawed by mice, coated with bat guano.

But they had. And they had stacked all of them in Mark's new bedroom, at the Ojeda house, earlier that morning.

Now Mark is transfixed. The boxes, neatly labeled in his Yiayia's handwriting, are full of his parents' papers. Bills, newspaper clippings, photos, medical records (lots of those), old report cards, you name it.

Both his parents had been very, very sick. The doctors had been baffled. The tumors had not been cancerous, but they were out of control, related to something called neurofibromatosis. Some doctors had conjectured his mom and dad had been exposed to harmful radiation levels; the odds of a husband and wife both developing so many tumors coincidentally were one in millions.

But what puzzles Mark the most is how they died. A few condolence letters to Yiayia refer to "mysterious circumstances," and a letter from some retired policeman apologizes for the "unexplained disappearances." Newspaper articles detail a court case against the same policeman for negligence. It seems he found the bodies — his mom's and dad's — but then they vanished. Poof.

Was it a murder? A crooked deal with the cop gone wrong? A double-suicide of two depressed, terminally ill people?

Was there any proof of death?

Mark hasn't even gone through a quarter of

the stuff when Walter Ojeda decides to wander in and demonstrate his concern.

"I can handle it," Mark says. "Shouldn't I know about my parents?"

"Of course," his foster father replies, looking around. "But . . . well, it's bound to be more depressing than enlightening, don't you think?"

"If I want to be depressed, that's my choice," Mark snaps. "All this stuff was kept from me. I have a right to see it."

Ojeda sits at the edge of the bed, near a box marked HIGH SCHOOL — 1990–1994. "I don't mean to be cruel," he says gently, "but it's in the past, Mark, and it belongs there."

"Okay, thanks, Mr. Ojeda — "

"Walter . . . or Dad, if you like."

"Thanks, Walter."

Mark watches the man walk from the room. Ojeda looks nervous, as if he expects a rat to jump out of one of the boxes.

As the door shuts, Mark opens one of the boxes on his bed.

Inside are four yearbooks — freshman, sophomore, junior, senior — in perfect condition.

PART NINE

David

Chapter 26

My eyes blinked open. The people in my dream — all familiar, yet all so strange — faded away.

Under me was a floor of hardened, slimy muck — the same yellowish stuff from which the tentacles were made. Distant walls rose around me, sweating yellow fluid. The smoke seemed to cling to the walls, rising upward to an opening I could not see.

Ariana was beside me, limp and unconscious. Her clothes were ripped, her backpack covered with slime.

I cradled her in my arms. She was breathing, and a hard lump had sprouted just below her left ear.

"Ariana," I whispered.

She groaned, nestling her head into my chest.

"A lovely couple, indeed."

I looked toward the voice.

Not far from Ariana and me, a sturdy column loomed high, rising out of the floor like a tree trunk. In front of it was a thin crack in the floor's surface. At the top, the column branched into three parts. On each branch sat a person — an older white man, a young white woman, and a teenaged black man. Each wore an identical, plain robe. Their smiles were grotesque, distorted by the lumps that covered their faces.

"Jonas Lyte," I said. "Annabelle Spicer . . . Reggie Borden. . . ."

The crack in the ground belched smoke.

"*Ehhhhh!* You have answered the identity question!" That was Reggie, imitating a talkshow host.

Jonas Lyte gave him a stern look.

Reggie shrugged. "Hey, I picked up a lot when I was aboveground. I would have been a great *Jeopardy* contestant."

Once again, smoke billowed from the crack.

"Okay, okay," Reggie said. "I'll shut up."

"It's . . . speaking to you!" I said. "The smoke . . . *that's* what you interpret."

The three looked at each other and nodded. "You are off to a good start," Annabelle Spicer replied.

Ariana began to stir. Her eyes flickered

open. "Oh . . . my . . . God. . . . Where am I?" She shot me a glance. "David!"

I hugged her tightly.

"How did it *taste*, Ariana?" Reggie asked. "No one has ever bitten Pytho before."

Ariana gasped. Annabelle and Jonas were glaring at Reggie. More smoke erupted.

"Pytho," I repeated.

Trembling, Ariana murmured, "Who are these jokers?"

"You may call us priests," Annabelle replied.

"I know, we don't look it," Reggie said with a sigh. "The collars are at the laundry."

"What do you want from us?" I asked.

"Not *us*, exactly," Jonas answered. "We need one of you. We had planned for that one to be you, Mr. Kallas."

"What about me?" Ariana said.

The three priests exchanged a glance.

I didn't wait for them to answer. "It meant to devour you, like Jason and John and Rick. It murders by student numbers on the alphabetical list of seniors. That was one of the clues it gave us. You were next in the sequence, but you threw it off by biting it."

"Hear! Hear!" Jonas cried. He began applauding, and the other two joined in.

I pulled the student list from my backpack and showed Ariana. "Look . . . the numbers double. Rick is 11, John is 22, Jason is 44, and you're 88 — "

Ariana grabbed the list and flipped back to the first page. "David, wait. Look who's behind John Christopher on the list. Number 21."

"Laura Chase . . ." *Pity, pity, Laura Chase,* her yearbook poem had begun.

"And here! Number 43, before Jason Herman — and 87."

Number 43 was Butthead Heald. Number 87, the student before Ariana Maas, was Ed Lyman.

"The yearbook poems," I muttered. "Every killing is off by one."

"Every one *except Rick Arnold*!" Ariana replied. "Don't you see?"

I didn't.

"David, do you remember why I hired you for the yearbook?"

"Of course," I said. "You needed someone to replace Sonya Eggert."

Ariana nodded. "And what happened to the student numbers when Sonya moved?"

I grabbed the list and flipped to the *E* section.

Sonya's name was missing, but the numbering continued uninterrupted.

"Everybody after Eggert moved up," I said.

"Right! The poems must have been written from the old list. This . . . this creature — Pytho — was being up to date."

The three priests roared their approval.

"Excellent!" Annabelle cried.

"Then why weren't the poems rewritten for the right people?" I asked.

"Because whoever sabotaged the book screwed up — " Ariana gasped. "Of course! How could we have been so stupid? *Mr. DeWaart* did it! He was the last to handle the layout before it got to Mr. Brophy's. He must have switched the photos and the poems in his car! When the yearbooks came out, he pretended to get all indignant and lied about Brophy. He's like . . . your *slave*."

The three cheered again. Reggie whistled wildly. "She's smarter than you, Kallas."

I was a little insulted. I *had* suspected Mr. DeWaart before.

"It's rare to find a sacrifice who may also qualify as a priest," Jonas remarked.

"Qualify as a priest?" Ariana looked horrified. "Wait a minute . . ."

Reggie quickly spoke up. "Okay, enough chitchat. Time's a-wastin'. You-know-who is pretty bugged about the biting. If you don't speak up, you could *both* be sacrificed. Dig? Nobody's sacred down here, pal. Okay, now here's the sixty-four-thousand-dollar question — who *is* this smoky knucklehead beneath us?"

"Pytho," I mumbled.

"You already know that," Jonas interjected.

Three pairs of eyes stared at us intently. In the silence, the smoke was starting to abate, as if Pytho were holding its breath. Strains of singing floated down from above. The Delphic Club was still at that same stupid song.

Delphic.

Delphi.

An oracle lived there. . . . Songs were sung day and night. . . .

Quickly I flipped the student list over and looked at the time line I had drawn:

1994 1950 1862 1686 1334 630 778 BC.

That last date seemed to jump off the page. "Pytho wasn't always in America," I said.

Annabelle smiled. "Go on."

"She was once in Ancient Greece," I went on. "In Delphi. Under a crack in the earth. Her messages were interpreted then, too. By a priestess."

The three priests stared silently. Ariana was gaping.

"And The Delphic Club — you *use* them.

Like the singers in Ancient Greece. Pytho's *entertainment*. They start their meetings, then the smoke changes them. And later they don't remember a thing. . . . "

All three nodded solemnly.

I held up my time line to the three priests. "For some reason Pytho seems to rest for years, then emerge. But each rest is half as long as the one before. And when Pytho wakes, she takes someone. All three of you died mysteriously, in a year Pytho awoke!"

Ariana smiled at me. "You figured that out?"

All three priests grinned their distorted, lumpy grins. "You passed the test of mental agility, David," Jonas said. "Both of you seem worthy — "

The ground gave up several puffs of smoke. Reggie, Jonas, and Annabelle all began to look uncomfortable.

"We can have only one priest," Annabelle said.

Ariana grabbed my arm.

Smoke poured out of the crack.

"Separate, please," Jonas said calmly.

"We won't!" Ariana retorted.

Ariana's arm was shaking (or maybe it was mine). I grabbed her tighter.

RRRRRRROMMMMM!

The ground shook. We both fell, letting go of each other.

"Don't make him into one of you!" Ariana shouted.

"We may not," Annabelle replied.

Ariana and I looked at each other. "Are you . . . going to let us go?" I asked.

"No," Reggie said. "One of you stays with us, one doesn't. Kids, it's immortality . . . or lunch. And guess what? Pytho wants it to be your choice."

Chapter 27

Sweat was pouring down my brow, stinging my eyes.

I looked at Ariana. Her face was pale and haggard, streaked with tears. She reached out to me. "David?"

Her fingers were icicles. I took them and drew her closer.

With a sudden spasm, the ground lurched again.

"Let go of each other!" Reggie demanded.

I held her tighter. Rage welled up within me. Through clenched teeth, I said, "Go to hell, Reggie."

A blast from below knocked us off our feet. We tumbled away from each other. Around us fell broken chunks of the wall.

I landed on my back, which was now ridged with bumps the size of ball bearings.

"Decide now!" Reggie shouted.

"David!" Ariana cried.

"Hold me!" I said. "Our togetherness hurts her."

We struggled to our feet and clutched each other. "You decide, Pytho," I shouted. "Which one of us should die?"

BOOOOOOOOMMMMM!

It felt as if an atom bomb had exploded. The priests' column split.

As the three of them held on, the smoke screened them from our view. Clouds gathered around us, thickening to the consistency of gelatin.

Then, slowly, Ariana and I began to rise.

We both screamed. What we could see of the wall was crumbling, falling. Flakes of it embedded themselves into our platform.

We clung to each other. Our rise was slow and unsteady. We heard Jonas's voice boom out: "When the pain gets too great — when the growths are too much to endure — only Pytho will be able to save you. And then you will come back. Begging."

Pytho's roar became more distant, until it was a low, agonized drone.

My fear was lifting. Relief washed over me like a summer rain. When the ledge came into view, we could see two figures peering over.

"David! Ariana!"

First we made out Chief Hayes's face. A moment later we saw the other person: Mr. Sarro, slack-jawed, clutching a can of Coca-Cola with both hands.

"What the — " Chief Hayes said. "Can you kids walk? Are you all right? How did you — what — "

Mr. Sarro's hands were trembling. Cola spurted from his can and fell to the ground. It landed on a broken-off chunk of Pytho's wall, which sizzled. "Wh-what happened to their faces?" he stammered.

"Oh, no," Ariana moaned. Her face was now covered with lumps. I ran my fingers over my own face and felt my heart sink.

When the growths are too much to endure . . .

"Never mind," Chief Hayes said. "Let's get out of here. If there's another tremor like that last one, I don't want to be under this building."

Holding hands, Ariana and I followed Chief Hayes and Mr. Sarro.

Pytho was quiet now, and the air had cleared somewhat. As we wound through the basement, Chief Hayes called over his shoulder, "You're lucky I found you. I was called to a fender-bender down the road. Some kid jumped into a busy street, then tore off for the high school, according to a witness. The rest was cop's intuition. I met Mr. Sarro when I got here."

"DeWaart was running upstairs with these kids in costumes!" Mr. Sarro said. He struggled to steady his hand as he took a swig of soda.

A few more drops spilled to the ground. They hit another chunk of Pytho's wall, and the chunk bubbled.

Ariana stopped. She was watching the bubbles intensely. When she looked up, her eyes were on fire.

"Guess what, guys?" she said. "We're going back there."

"Are you nuts?" I replied. "We'll be killed."

"No we won't." Ariana grinned wildly. "We'll be armed."

Chapter 28

"This looks absolutely ridiculous," Chief Hayes muttered.

We sped down the deserted street. The trunk was ajar, holding seven cases of Coke and Pepsi with the help of a rope.

The backseat held another six cases of two-liter bottles, the back window ledge another one, and the floor two more. If you added the one case on my lap, and the twenty-one in Mr. Sarro's van, that made thirty-six cases.

We were lucky to get them. The A&P had been about to close. After the last tremor, people were gathering in open fields — away from trees, cars, and buildings.

On the way to the supermarket I had explained everything I knew to Chief Hayes — including Reggie Borden's role. He hadn't thought I was crazy. He had just nodded grimly and agreed with our plan.

Ariana had the job of convincing Mr. Sarro. Judging from the grin she gave me from the window of the van, everything had gone fine.

As for the Coca-Cola, well, she hadn't wanted to explain in the supermarket, because she was afraid we would laugh at her. We just had to trust her.

At this point, nothing seemed too weird to try.

Mr. Sarro pulled into the school parking lot first. As we parked, he ran inside and Ariana opened the van doors.

"Ready, guys?" she called out.

"Ready for *what*?" Chief Hayes demanded, stepping out of the car. "We did what you wanted. Will you explain why we're doing this — and slowly, so my aging brain can understand?"

"Okay." Ariana thought for a moment. "What is the major substance in the human body?"

Chief Hayes rolled his eyes. "*Water*. Everybody knows that. What does that have to do with — "

"The body is over ninety percent water," Ariana went on. "We need to drink it all the time in order to survive. Now, supposing we imagine another life-form. For *its* survival it needs something just as intensely, but some *other* substance besides water."

"I assume you're talking about this . . . Pytho," Chief Hayes said.

Ariana nodded. "You noticed the smell down there — "

"Chalky," Chief Hayes replied.

"Right!" Ariana said.

"It needs *chalk* to survive?" I asked.

"No, David," Ariana groaned. "Look, how did you describe Rick Arnold's body to me?"

"It looked as if something had sucked the bones right out — "

"And what do bone and chalk have in common?"

"Calcium," I murmured. "They're made of calcium."

"Or some form of it," Ariana said. "Pytho is a calcium freak. Her tentacles, the walls around her, they're all made of it. She takes it from her human sacrifices — "

"Yeah, but if Pytho's as big as you say, she'd have to kill the whole town to get enough," Chief Hayes said.

Ariana shrugged. "I didn't say I knew where she got it all."

"From the soil," I said.

"Huh?" Ariana and Chief Hayes both stared at me.

"It was in one of the articles I saved from 1950," I said. "The soil was depleted of calcium, and no one knew why."

We all looked toward the worn-out football field. "Sort of hard to know by looking, huh?" Chief Hayes remarked.

"I'll bet if somebody measured right now, the soil would have the same problem," Ariana suggested.

"Okay, genius," I said, "so how do you explain these bony growths on all of us?"

Ariana shook her head. "I'm not sure. I think some part of Pytho — some weird germ or virus — is getting into our systems through the smoke. It affects whatever makes calcium in our own bodies."

"Uh, before you completely lose me," Chief Hayes said, "can we get back to this Coca-Cola business?"

"Have you ever put a tooth in a glass of cola, Chief Hayes?" Ariana asked.

"Uh, can't say I have," he replied. "Not recently."

"Well, if you do, the tooth will disintegrate."

"Something to do with the reaction of calcium with the carbonation and the acidity of the Coke," I said.

Ariana stared at me. "How do *you* know?"

I shrugged. "Chemistry, I guess."

Chief Hayes nodded. "And when Mr. Sarro spilled some of his Coke on that piece of slate . . ."

"*Fsssshtt,*" Ariana said.

Mr. Sarro came out the back door with a long rope slung over his shoulder. He was rolling four hand trucks. On one of them was a cardboard box and a gasoline can. "We ready?" he called out.

A smile spread across Chief Hayes's face. "Let's go for it."

We managed to load up the trucks with cola cases. Slowly we wheeled them into the school, then brought them backstage and carefully lowered them into the scenery shop.

As we pushed the bulky trucks through the bookcase opening, Mr. Sarro stared wide-eyed at the walls. "Jeez," he said, "I think I wrote some of this stuff."

Chief Hayes nodded toward one of the drawings. "Yeah, but no one drew a picture of *you.*"

In a darkened area, half-hidden by scribbling, was a caricature of two basketball players, one ridiculously tall and skinny, the other squat and fat.

Underneath were the words: FIRST THE MASS. CHAMPIONSHIP, THEN THE NBA! It was signed Charlie Hayes and Reggie Borden.

Chief Hayes's head lowered. "Ah, well. Life doesn't always work out the way you expect."

The hand-truck wheels squeaked over the dirt floor. "Are you sure you want to do this?" I finally asked. "He was your best buddy. . . ."

Chief Hayes held out a hand to quiet me. "My best buddy is dead," he said. "The person you described was in Reggie's body, but it was nothing like him."

None of us said a word as we rolled the cases deeper into the basement.

As we got closer to the crack, the smoke began to swirl again. The ground beneath us thrummed. Mr. Sarro mumbled a prayer.

Soon we were able to see the crack clearly. A mist spewed out, steady and rhythmic, but not nearly as thick as it had been.

"What now?" I whispered.

Ariana turned to Mr. Sarro. "Set it up, and show Chief Hayes what to do!"

"Yes, *ma'am*," he muttered.

Mr. Sarro began opening the cases and setting them on their sides, lined up against the edge of the crevice, with the caps pointing forward. He said something to Chief Hayes, who ripped open the cardboard box and started pulling out rags.

I watched him lay out the rags behind the boxes, and looked curiously at Ariana. "So what do we do, spill it and run away?"

She shook her head. "We may not need to. Remember how Pytho reacted when we held hands? She went ballistic. Something about that contact, that demonstration of . . . you know, *solidarity*, or — "

"Or what?" I asked.

"What?" Ariana repeated.

"I don't know . . . love?"

Ariana smiled. "Solidarity."

We were both turning red.

"Anyway," Ariana barged on, "I believe *that*'s our best weapon. We have to try that first. The other plan may not be strong enough."

"You mean, *go back in*? Are you crazy — "

"Sssshhh . . . David, a lot of people have died because of this thing. You came along and cracked the code. You were the only person who figured out what was happening in this town. If I had trusted you earlier, maybe together we could have saved Jason."

"Don't think about that — "

"No. I was too wrapped up in the yearbook, and Stephen, and all my stupid problems. But now I *know* what needs to be done, David. And I need you to trust me — enough to try this plan. Do you?"

I looked into her eyes. I had never trusted anyone as much in my life. "Yeah."

Ariana took a Coke bottle and put it in her pack. "Just in case," she said.

I took a deep breath. Together we walked to the edge of the crevice.

Chapter 29

Under us bubbled the putrid yellow-white mass of solid, liquid, gas.

"Yo! What the hell do you think you're doing?" Chief Hayes shouted behind us.

His footsteps pounded dully on the basement floor.

"We're ready, Pytho!" Ariana screamed into the crevice. *"If you want us, come and get us!"*

Chief Hayes grabbed my left arm. I resisted, but I was off-balance.

I didn't see what happened next. I was falling backward in the chief's vice grip.

But I heard Ariana's shattering scream. And I felt something clammy lash around my other arm.

For a moment, I thought the arm would rip off like a celery stalk. Instead, Chief Hayes let go — and my feet left the ground.

I saw Ariana beside me, flailing, borne on one thick, oozing tentacle.

Our eyes locked for a split second. Fear shot between us like lightning.

The tendrils lowered us quickly. My stomach lurched, and by the time we reached bottom, I was fighting the urge to puke.

We tumbled to the ground, a dozen or so yards from each other. The tendrils retracted into the smoking crevice in front of the three-seated column.

"Welcome!" Jonas's voice bellowed from above.

I did not look at him. I was staring at the tentacles. They looked different. The one that had carried me had two small black lesions. Ariana's looked as if someone had taken a chunk out of it.

One glance at Ariana, and I knew she had noticed, too.

"Hold me," she said, scrambling to her feet.

I ran toward her, arms open.

Rrrrommmmm!

A tentacle shot out of the small crack. It caught me on the jaw and sent me flying backward.

I saw Ariana reach into her backpack. She pulled out the bottle and opened it.

The tentacle whipped around her, tying her arms to her sides.

With her wrist, she tilted the bottle and let it spill.

TSSSSSSSSSSSS . . .

Smoke flashed from the tentacle. Ooze gushed upward. It stiffened, then unwound itself in one jerk.

Something beyond noise, deafening and unearthly, welled up from the crack. I felt it vibrate my bones, echo in the chambers of my body. The noise expressed pain so intense, it brought tears to my own eyes.

As the tentacle dragged itself back into the crack, Ariana raced over to me. We threw our arms around each other.

"That was dumb," Reggie Borden said. "Really colossally stupid."

"Have you both chosen to die?" Jonas asked. "Will neither of you join us?"

Ariana and I stepped toward the crack, ignoring the voices. "How long will you last," Ariana asked, "if we stay together against you?"

"Separate!" Jonas commanded.

"This will not work!" Annabelle cried. "Pytho will destroy you!"

I looked into the deep gash. Against the

steep wall, amid the roiling smoke, I could see a large, round pipe opening.

My breath caught in my throat. "That's where the bodies went," I murmured.

The rumbling began again. Ariana began tilting the bottle.

BOOOOOMM!

Suddenly the ground split between Ariana and me. Fighting to keep balance, we let go of each other.

"Ariana!"

She was reaching toward me. I extended my arm.

Our fingers locked. They stayed together for a second, then slipped.

I slid off the broken ledge. Desperately I grabbed for it. My hands slapped uselessly against the slimy surface.

I plunged downward, crying out at the top of my lungs.

Dark droplets fell around me from above. Some glanced against the wall, sizzling.

The smoke now blinded and choked me. I landed on my side and blacked out.

When my eyes opened, Ariana was beside me, grimacing with pain. The cola bottle was in pieces a few feet away. I reached out with aching arms and held her with all the strength I had left.

"Stop this nonsense!"

Reggie's voice was changing, becoming distorted and higher-pitched. Ariana and I glanced upward.

At the top of the tripod, the three priests were gyrating. Their movements were jerky and involuntary, as if cockroaches had crawled into their robes. Their eyes bulged, and their mouths seemed to be peeling backward, stretching across their faces.

"What's going on?" I called out.

"Leave Pytho . . . alone!" Reggie struggled to say. "Stop-op pouring the chemical-ical. Releasssssse each other. Pytho will go will go . . . back to ssssleep. She promises."

"And when will she return?" I asked. "What is it, twenty-two years from now? Then eleven? Ready to eat our kids? You think we want to let that happen?"

"Stop! Go 'way!"

The voice was Annabelle's, but the tone was like a baby's — pleading, almost crying.

Crrrack!

I jumped. A moldering chunk had fallen from the wall above, shattering at my feet.

Ariana and I looked up. The walls had become mottled with black and gray spots.

Reggie, Annabelle, and Jonas were now babbling in their seats. No, they were *attached* to their seats. Their feet had melded into the calcified stalk below them.

Ariana's arm tightened. "My god . . ." she murmured. "What is happening?"

As we watched, Reggie's face bulged in all directions. His ear pointed upward, then ruptured bloodlessly. A tendril emerged from his head, growing and twisting. It looked cancerous, chipped and covered with tiny lesions.

In an accelerating rhythm, tendrils ripped their way out of the other two.

"Yuth aaabba iggrashashasha rammmmahh . . ."

They were moving their mouths, oblivious to pain, spouting nonsense.

Ariana was turning green. "We're killing her," she said.

Slowly, a crooked and creaking tentacle rose out of the crevice. It hovered over our heads, its point flapping lifelessly. It grew, slowly winding and spiraling into a tight coil.

Then, suddenly, it lashed out with blinding force.

Ariana and I fell to the ground. The chamber jolted again and again. We bounced violently. My nose smashed into the floor.

When I sat up, I saw what the tentacle was attacking: the wall. With each thrust, it chopped a deep hole, higher and higher. It didn't stop until it was out of sight.

Then it fell silent. The tentacle lost its rigidity and fell back into the crevice with a tremendous crash.

I took Ariana's hand. Together we walked to the vertical holes. The lowest one was about four feet up.

"Come on," I said.

I gave Ariana a boost. She stepped into the foothold and began climbing.

Chapter 30

Chief Hayes and Mr. Sarro looked as if they were competing for widest mouth of the year. They stared at us silently, jaws hanging open. I wished I had some popcorn for target practice.

"Fine, thanks, how are you?" I said.

Chief Hayes shook his head once, twice. He unlocked his jaw. "I will suspend disbelief. I will not ask questions. This is my vow. Now, what do we do with these?"

He pointed to the cases of cola, still poised at the edge of the abyss.

Ariana and I took deep breaths. The smoke was wisping upward now in grayish-black puffs. Pytho's moans resounded.

"She's weak," I said.

"She's been weak before," Ariana replied. "I say go for it."

"Hallelujah!" Mr. Sarro blurted.

All of Mr. Sarro's rags were stuffed against the cardboard cases. Chief Hayes grimly spurted them with gasoline as we uncoiled the rope back through the basement.

It ended a few yards before the bookcase. Chief Hayes followed, dousing the rope itself with the fuel.

"Is the school empty?" Chief Hayes asked.

"Give me a few minutes," Mr. Sarro said. "I'll make sure."

The few minutes seemed eternal. We waited silently.

When Mr. Sarro came down, he was out of breath. "Not a soul."

Chief Hayes pulled a lighter out of his pocket. "You guys go up. I'll meet you."

"No," I said. "We'll do this together."

Chief Hayes looked defiant for a moment. Then he sighed. "All right. But I get to light it. I've got the longest grudge."

He flicked on the lighter and touched it to the rope.

The flame shot high. We bolted up the stairs and through the nearest exit. Mr. Sarro led us out of the school. Ariana grabbed my hand as we ran across the parking lot.

We were half a block away when the school blew for the first time.

The blast knocked us off our feet. I looked

back. The first floor was crumbling, and the school tilted. The air filled with smoke, black and sooty but with the faint odor of chalk.

I covered my mouth.

"This wasn't supposed to happen!" Ariana cried.

"Come on!" I shouted.

Holding her hand firmly, I ran for the hills on the south side of town. In the growing soot, Chief Hayes and Mr. Sarro were nowhere to be seen.

The sirens began immediately. Panic surrounded us. We wound our way through streets clogged with people.

Ariana was right. We had not planned to explode anything. The gasoline was used sparingly, to guide the flame. The burning rags were supposed to heat the bottles so the caps would shoot off. Pytho would be doused with the lethal liquid.

Pytho was supposed to decay to death. The school might sustain some damage — but not like this.

The soot was spreading over the town. Screams of "Fire!" rang out. As we ran up the hill, we heard sounds of smashing glass.

We didn't stop. Unfortunately, neither of us knew the hill well. We found a path but lost it.

Branches whipped against us, thorns ripped our clothes. We didn't say a word until we got to a clearing. The ground was rocky, the trees thin.

Below us, Wetherby lay under a cloud — gray and dusty, but tinged with yellow and white.

"Mom," I managed to say. "She's down there."

Ariana's eyes were bloodshot and despairing. "What did we do?" she whispered.

Tears welled up in my eyes. The bump on my forehead throbbed, and I rubbed it. "I don't know. Maybe it's all a dream."

We sat there in silence for a long time. I expected — wanted — "The End" to appear across my field of vision. Like a movie.

Ariana buried her head in my chest and began to sob. I was strangely numb. It hadn't sunk in.

Still hasn't.

I knew Ariana and I might be the only ones to survive this. Was it worth the price? And how long did we have to live? Pytho had warned us our sores would bind us to her. Did that mean we died when she did? Had we killed her? Had we done what thousands of years could not do?

As darkness began to fall, prematurely,

Ariana sank onto the grass and fell asleep. But I couldn't. I reached into my pack and pulled out my pack of legal pads.

And now I'm finished. I have included everything. Ariana has awakened and helped me remember. We'll head down soon. The smoke is clearing, and there is movement. Sound. Life.

We will decide what to do when we get there. We'll save this journal. I don't know what we'll do with it.

But whatever we do, we'll do it together.

That is the only thing in my life I'm sure of.

PART TEN

Mark

Chapter 31

It's after midnight. Walter Ojeda is snoring.

Mark flicks on his night-light. He reaches into the box and pulls out the yearbook marked 1991.

He sees his dad as a freshman, lumped in with his homeroom class. He looks a little nerdy, but his face is clear. None of those scars left by the plastic surgeon who had done such a lousy jobs on that bone disease.

Mom's in another class, and she looks gorgeous and confident.

Neither of them had the disease then. Mark has always thought they'd met at the doctor's office, fallen in love because of the neurofibromatosis they had in common.

He finishes the book and puts it down. Then he picks up their senior book. The important one. 1994. Twenty-two years ago.

But there is no yearbook inside. The pages

have been ripped out. In their place is a stack of brown-edged legal papers.

He picks up the top one and reads his dad's writing:

My name is David Kallas.

I am in trouble.

I do not know how long I will live.

My only possessions are the clothes I'm wearing and my backpack, which contains this pen and pad.

I do not know if my mother and my house still exist.

What's more, I have a splitting head-ache. . . .

Epilogue

Mark steps out of the elevator. He walks into the basement of the Wetherby Chemical plant.

In his hand is a sheet of paper. At the top is written the name WALTER OJEDA. Below it is line after line of crossouts, ending with another name, in angry black letters:

JOEL DEWAART.

Mark walks into the darkness. The mist is beginning to swirl, but he expects that.

And he is not surprised to see the four silhouettes emerging from the vapor. He barely notices the stooped black man, the ancient white guy holding the soda can.

But he can't help staring at the other two. The man and woman whose distorted faces are streaked with tears, whose smiles border on joyous madness.

The words push through his parched lips: "Mom . . . Dad?"

David and Ariana Kallas open their arms.

Mark runs toward them. Their embrace takes away the pain, the snakelike grip that has smothered him most of his life.

"We . . . had to leave you," David says, his voice choked with emotion.

"I know," Mark replies. "I read what you wrote."

Mark knows everything now. That the infections became a kind of cancer. That his parents would have died if they hadn't returned to Pytho — to be preserved in her healing sleep, to be reclaimed at the awakening. It was just as the monster had warned them.

But Mark also knows that Pytho sent him a test. She sent him DeWaart.

She wants Mark, too.

Mark sees the cloud swirl around them. He knows it's time.

Fear grips him, fear that his parents have been transformed.

But their eyes tell him something else. Pytho does not have them.

Not yet.

"I don't know if we can fight back this time," Ariana says wearily.

Mark looks toward the smoking gash. "There are three of us now."

"Five," says the old police chief behind them.
Mr. Sarro grunts in agreement.

They move together and hold hands tightly.
The smoke circles them, taking their breath
away, pushing them apart.

But Mark will not let go.

None of them will.

Ever.

Point Horror

Also in the Point Horror series:

The Cemetery
D.E. Athkins

The Dead Game
Mother's Helper
A. Bates

The Cheerleader
The Vampire's Promise
The Return of the Vampire
Freeze Tag
The Perfume
The Stranger
Twins
Caroline B. Cooney

April Fools
The Lifeguard
Teacher's Pet
Trick or Treat
Richie Tankersley Cusick

Camp Fear
My Secret Admirer
The Window
Carol Ellis

The Accident
The Invitation
Funhouse
The Fever
The Train
Diane Hoh

Nightmare Hall:
A Silent Scream
Deadly Attraction
The Roommate
The Wish
Diane Hoh

The Watcher
Lael Littke

Dream Date
The Diary
The Waitress
Sinclair Smith

The Phantom
Barbara Steiner

The Baby-sitter
The Baby-sitter II
The Baby-sitter III
Beach House
Beach Party
The Boyfriend
Call Waiting
The Dead Girlfriend
The Girlfriend
Halloween Night
The Hitchhiker
Hit and Run
The Snowman
The Witness
R.L. Stine

Thirteen Tales of Horror
Thirteen More Tales of Horror
Various

Point Horror Fans Beware!

Available now from Point Horror are tales
for the midnight hour...

THE *Point Horror* TAPES

Two Point Horror stories are terrifyingly
brought to life in a chilling dramatisation
featuring actors from The Story Circle and
with spine tingling sound effects.

Point Horror as you've never heard
it before...

HALLOWEEN NIGHT
FUNHOUSE

available now on audiotape at your
nearest bookshop.

Listen if you dare...

Point Romance

If you like Point Horror, you'll love Point Romance!

Anyone can hear the language of love.

Are you burning with passion, and aching with desire? Then these are the books for you! Point Romance brings you passion, romance, heartache . . . and *love*.

Available now:

First Comes Love:
To Have and to Hold
For Better, For Worse
In Sickness and in Health
Till Death Do Us Part
Jennifer Baker

A Winter Love Story
Jane Claypool Miner

Two Weeks in Paradise
Denise Colby

Saturday Night
Last Dance
New Year's Eve
Summer Nights
Caroline B. Cooney

Cradle Snatcher
Kiss Me, Stupid
Alison Creaghan

Summer Dreams, Winter Love
Mary Francis Shura

The Last Great Summer
Carol Stanley

Lifeguards:
Summer's Promise
Summer's End
Todd Strasser

French Kiss
Robyn Turner

Look out for:

Crazy About You
Robyn Turner

Spotlight on Love
Denise Colby

Last Summer, First Love:
A Time to Love
Goodbye to Love
Jennifer Baker